"I take it you're not the housewarming present the guys promised me?" he inquired.

"Excuse me?" Megan got out.

"Boomer, Rick, and Coney," he clarified calmly. "When they gave me these sheets"—he indicated the satin bedclothes with a deprecating gesture—"they hinted there might be something . . . special . . . to go with them."

The brief but pointed pauses bracketing the adjective obviously were meant to provoke. So, no doubt, was the brief but pointed up-down assessment of his remarkable eyes.

"Mr. Swann," she said through gritted teeth. "Mr. Swann, whatever the other members of Nightshade were hinting about, *I* am *not* it!"

"Somehow, I didn't think so," he remarked. "It's too bad, though. I have the feeling you'd be very good at warming a . . . ah . . . house."

Carole Buck

Born on the Fourth of July, Carole Buck was raised in Connecticut and now makes her home in Atlanta. Although she had ambitions to be a ballerina, a lawyer, an archaeologist, and a spy, she somehow ended up as a television news writer and entertainment reporter. She spends a lot of time in the dark, because she is also a movie reviewer. Her greatest fantasy is to travel back in time.

Carole is single. She says her men friends are always offering to help her do research for her romance novels. Her women friends want introductions to the heroes she writes about. Carole just wishes her characters would remember she's supposed to be in charge.

Life, says Carole, is a banquet, and she intends to fill her plate to the fullest as many times as she can.

Dear Reader:

Here, just for you, is a spring bouquet of six new SECOND CHANCE AT LOVE romances.

Prolific Carole Buck is one of my favorites—and one of yours, too, judging from the enthusiastic response we receive for her endearingly humorous, emotionally charged love stories. In *Swann's Song* (#334) we meet irrepressible Megan Harper, who wakes up in bed with seminaked rock star Colin Swann—and no recollection of how she got there! At heart *Swann's Song* is a delightfully domestic tale. You see, Megan's posing as nanny to "Swann's" son P.J., so she gets to see Swann far outside his rock milieu—as a man who fulfills his family responsibilities with devastating warmth and wit. As Swann's secret bodyguard, Megan's real job is to stay intimately close to him—no tough task, believe me! But she knows she'll be in big trouble when he learns of her deception—and is she ever! *Swann's Song* is another fresh, original winner from Carole Buck.

Does crime ever pay? It sure does—in the form of a sinfully delicious romance, *Stolen Kisses* (#335), by the inimitable Liz Grady. Our captivating "culprits" are novice cat burglar Mathilda Sprague Hamilton (by day, a respectable jewelry-firm president) and Devlin Seamus Devlin, the debonair, tuxedo-clad professional thief who'll bend any rule to keep feisty Mattie on the straight and narrow. Brace yourself for one of romance's most seductive rogues, because as he's stealing kisses from Mattie, he's bound to steal your heart! Wise, witty, and wonderful, *Stolen Kisses* is truly a "hot" property.

In Jacqueline Topaz's newest romance, *Golden Girl* (#336), we meet a heroine who comes looking for adventure and discovers it in abundance! Olivia Gold considers herself just an ordinary schoolteacher, but when she arrives in Hollywood to seek out her grandmother, a famous silver-screen star, she undergoes an exciting transformation into a glittering golden girl. *And* she falls in love with breathtaking Andrew Carr—the one man who sees past all the surface shine to her sensitive woman's heart. Here's another fast-paced story from a writer whose work is always full of exciting surprises.

Do you sometimes miss those wonderfully cynical, supremely arrogant, dashingly brooding heroes of yesteryear? The kind who smoothly seduced innocent governesses under moonlit magnolias? Well, weep no more, ladies: Dashing plantation owner Jules Robichaux is here—and nanny April Jasper has her hands full, trying to cope with his orphaned niece and nephew *and* with Jules's tantalizingly brazen charm. In *Smiles of a*

Summer Night (#337), Delaney Devers weaves a spell as Southern as hominy, as dangerously sultry as a Louisiana summer ... and then leaves us with smiles as refreshing as a dewy morning. Rhett Butler, move over!

What new romance combines astrology, football, X-rated Easter eggs, *and* a charity benefit at which Dot Biancardi is auctioned off to her ex-husband, Bart Easton? Why, *Destiny's Darling* (#338) by husband and wife team Adrienne Edwards, of course! With a light, deft touch these new writers for SECOND CHANCE AT LOVE tell a classic tale of a reformed hero's efforts to win back the woman he shouldn't ever have let go. No hero has ever pursued a heroine so inventively. No heroine has ever resisted so valiantly. You'll be captivated as Dot and Bart recall memories of their past, both funny and bittersweet, and struggle to build a future, in this endearing romance by writers whose work you'll be seeing more of.

Finally this month, Lee Williams brings you *Wild and Wonderful* (#339), a romance about loved ones lost and found. Heir hunter Alicia Saunders journeys to a rugged Maine island to find Greg Bowles, a burly man's man with heart-melting eyes and indomitable strength, who rejects the inheritance she's come to give him ... just as he once rejected his wealthy, snobbish family. In finding each other, Alicia and Greg discover within themselves untapped capacities for loving. Traveling across the continent to a palatial mansion and on to the Louisiana bayou, they set out to reconcile their pain-filled pasts. *Wild and Wonderful* is a poignant and passionate exploration of a relationship forged from a sometimes heart-wrenching coming to terms ... Keep a hanky handy!

And if you can, please do take time from your busy day to drop us a line about this month's books. We love hearing from you!

Warm wishes,

Ellen Edwards

Ellen Edwards, Senior Editor
SECOND CHANCE AT LOVE
The Berkley Publishing Group
200 Madison Avenue
New York, NY 10016

SECOND CHANCE AT LOVE

CAROLE BUCK
SWANN'S SONG

A
SECOND CHANCE AT LOVE
BOOK

Second Chance at Love books are published by
The Berkley Publishing Group
200 Madison Avenue, New York, NY 10016

To my editor, Janet Kronstadt,
who always makes it better

CHAPTER ONE

AT AGE THIRTY, Megan Louise Harper had had a certain amount of experience with getting herself into—and out of—trouble. In some ways, it was fair to say that trouble was her business, her *family* business. Simply put: It took a lot to throw Megan Harper.

How much?

Well, waking up to discover that she was in an unfamiliar room, in an unfamiliar bed, wearing nothing but a very large and unfamiliar T-shirt was enough to unsettle her more than a little. Add to all that the fact that there was a seminaked rock star propped up on one elbow beside her—

"Hello," the seminaked rock star said. His voice was velvet-rich with an intriguingly husky rasp around the edges. A frisson of awareness danced along Megan's spine as he followed up the greeting with a slow, sexy smile. The smile could have melted the polar ice caps.

And the way he was looking at her! During the first

few seconds Megan stared into his unusual, silver-grey eyes, she thought he might be as uncertain about this situation as she was, that he was trying to make up his mind what he wanted to do. Then something distinctly and dangerously male stirred in the depths of his lustrous gaze, unmistakably informing her that he knew precisely what he wanted to do. It was only a matter of deciding where he wanted to begin.

The dark, strongly marked brows that arched arrogantly over his unique, heavily lidded eyes lifted slightly. "Hello?" he repeated. "Anyone home in there?"

"Uh—" Megan swallowed hard. Her tongue felt as though it had spent the night wrapped in an old sweat sock. She swallowed again, trying to order the thoughts that were rattling inside her skull like loose marbles. "Uh—good morning."

Maybe . . . maybe this is some kind of dream? she suggested to herself hopefully. You've had weird dreams before, Megan, remember? Like the one with Mickey Mouse at the Eiffel Tower? Well, maybe this is just another one of those! You don't really believe this is happening, do you?

Unfortunately, she did.

And Lord, she could just imagine what her younger brother, Kyle, would say when—no, *if* he ever found out about this! Kyle, overprotective sibling and experienced undercover operative that he was, had had some reservations about her inclusion in this particular assignment. But her father, as head of Harper Security, Incorporated, had decided she was just what the job needed.

Just what the job needed. Right. She'd blown her role in this case before she'd ever really gotten into the part!

And speaking of getting into things . . . just how in the name of heaven had she ended up in a totally unfamiliar room that was unfurnished except for a black satin-sheeted bed the size of the state of Rhode Island?

More to the point, how had she ended up in that bed

with Colin Swann—Good Lord, *Colin Swann!*—lying next to her?

Colin Swann. Tall, dark, and devastatingly attractive. Lead singer and guitarist for Nightshade, a musical group so hot it was radioactive.

Colin Swann. A member of Hollywood's aristocracy by birth. A member of rock royalty by achievement.

Colin Swann. The man Harper Security, Incorporated, had been secretly hired to protect. The man *she'd* been assigned to get close to, but not this close!

"So, you *can* talk," Swann murmured conversationally, breaking in on her train of thought. Again, she felt a small quiver of awareness at the sound of his voice—as though her body were especially attuned to it. He shifted himself slightly, a provocative glimmer appearing in his compelling eyes. "Good morning to you, too," he said. "A *very* good morning."

And then he kissed her.

At first, the kiss was whisper-light, more a mingling of breaths than an actual touching of lips. But, as fleeting as the initial contact was, it sent a shivery tingle of anticipation flowing through Megan.

The flow cascaded into a flood of feelings as Swann deepened the kiss by teasing, tantalizing increments. The expertly erotic movements of his mouth were sweetly, searingly suggestive—full of passionate innuendo.

The silken search of his lips and tongue complemented the sleek friction of the satin sheets as they rubbed against her body. The fabric was deliciously cool and sensuously soft . . . like a lover's touch.

A moment later, she felt the faintly abrasive yet arousing brush of crisp body hair against her slender legs. This was followed by the insinuating stroke of slightly callused fingertips along her thigh.

The fingertips moved upward. Slowly . . . searchingly—

Megan jerked herself away from him and sat up like

a jack-in-the-box. She was shaking with reaction. Her red-gold curls bounced around her skull like electrified marmalade.

The very large and unfamiliar T-shirt she was wearing was purple and carried the Nightshade logo scrawled across the front. It was also slipping off her shoulders. Megan yanked it back into place, glaring at her bed partner.

"Just what do you think you're doing?" she demanded.

Colin Swann sat up beside her in a lean, liquid display of pantherlike muscularity. His skin was deeply tanned. A triangle of dark, slightly curly hair arrowed down his broad chest.

The austere clarity of his chiseled features—which was emphasized, not softened, by the casual disorder of his longish pitch-black hair—was overlaid with a mixture of amusement and wary intelligence. His wide-set eyes were like mirrors: reflecting, deflecting, eating the light.

"Well?" she prompted.

"I take it you're not the housewarming present the guys promised me?" he inquired.

"Excuse me?" she got out. Although she could feel her blood pressure soaring, she was glad to hear that her voice remained steady.

Her hands remained steady, too, al long as she kept them clenched into fists.

"Boomer, Rick, and Coney," he clarified calmly. "When they gave me these sheets"—he indicated the satin bedclothes with a deprecating gesture—"they hinted there might be something . . . special . . . to go with them."

The brief but pointed pauses bracketing the adjective obviously were meant to provoke. So, no doubt, was the brief but pointed up-down assessment of his remarkable eyes.

What Megan privately classed as one of the two curses of the fair-skinned redhead struck: She flushed a deep scarlet.

"Mr. Swann," she said through gritted teeth. "Mr. Swann, whatever the other members of Nightshade were hinting about, *I* am *not* it!"

"Somehow, I didn't think so," he remarked. "It's too bad, though." Except for a barely perceptible quirking of his lips, there was no indication that he'd registered her use of his name or her identification of the three men he'd mentioned.

"Too bad?" Megan edged back, wishing she wasn't so conscious of his insistent physicality.

"Mmm," he murmured, his expression reflective. "I have the feeling you'd be very good at warming a . . . ah . . . house."

Megan sucked in her breath. "Look," she said tautly, fighting for control. She was struggling against the other curse of the fair-skinned redhead: a hot temper. "Look, will you please just tell me how I—if we—*what happened last night?*"

Swann cocked his head. "Don't you know?"

"Do you think I'd be asking if I did?"

Oh, dear Lord, why couldn't she remember what had gone on between them? She could recall the first part of the previous evening well enough to give sworn testimony about it. But at a certain point—*boom!* Lights out.

"Will you feel better if I give you my word that I don't kiss and tell?" Swann asked. "Despite what you may read in the tabloids."

"Wha—*no!*" Megan erupted, feeling a new wave of hot blood rush up into her cheeks. His teasing question opened the door on several dozen appalling possibilities. "Mr. Swann—"

"Just Swann," he corrected.

"I—what?"

"Swann. No Mister. Colin, if you prefer. Although nobody but my mother calls me that. Still—"

"All right. *Swann*. Look, will you please just tell me—"

"And you're—?" he cut in smoothly.

Megan blinked. *And I'm about to become unglued!* she wanted to scream at him. Maybe Colin Swann was used to waking up with someone he couldn't remember having gone to bed with, but she wasn't. She couldn't even remember having been properly introduced to this man! She wanted explanations, not an exercise in morning-after-the-night-before etiquette.

"You don't remember your name, either?" he inquired.

"Of course, I remember my name!"

"Then?" He made a prompting gesture with his right hand. It was the same hand he'd used to touch her when—

"Megan!" she answered hastily, not wanting to think about that particular memory. "My name is Megan."

For a split second, she had the impression the name meant something to him. She swiftly discarded the idea. Colin Swann didn't know her from Adam—or Eve!

"Megan." He pronounced the name as though savoring its flavor. The husky rasp that threaded through his velvety voice transformed the two syllables into a celebration of sensuality.

Megan felt herself tremble. She might be upset and angry, and she might be concerned about letting down the agency, but she wasn't immune to the power of that voice—or to the sheer animal magnetism of the man who possessed it. Her susceptibility was as unnerving as it was unexpected. She'd been distinctly wary of the male sex since the breakup of her marriage and her divorce from Doug Carlyle a year ago.

Her family, she knew, was anxious about her aloofness. They'd all tried—with differing degrees of subtlety—to encourage her to get back into the social swing of things.

The social swing of things. Lord! She may have experienced her first one-night stand . . . but she had no memory of it!

"Swann." She licked her lips. "I—about what happened . . . between us." Spit it out, Megan, she ordered. You're sitting here in bed with this man. You're past the point of coyness. "You said—I mean, did you and I—did we—?"

He cut short her embarrassed verbal floundering with a single word: "No."

"No?" One of the things she'd learned in her line of work was to be absolutely certain of her facts. Especially in a touchy situation.

"No."

"Thank goodness," she said feelingly, exhaling a gusty sigh. She slumped a little, going limp as a Raggedy Ann doll. The burden of her unanswered questions about the previous night still weighed on her, but the anxiety was a little less heavy than before.

"Your reaction isn't very flattering, you know," Swann observed dryly after a few seconds of silence.

"My what?" she echoed uncertainly, her head coming up. The T-shirt had started slipping again. She shrugged it back into place.

"Your obvious relief that we didn't make love."

Megan exhaled, the sound falling somewhere between a gasp of indignation and a snort of disbelief. Oh, she was perfectly aware of Colin Swann's reputation as a lover. Even if the agency hadn't been given a very thorough dossier on his background, she would have had to have been living in a cave in Tasmania not to know about Colin Swann. The man's amorous activities were front page, headline material. But still! Was he so sexually arrogant that he expected her to react with regret to his statement that they'd hadn't made love?

"Of course, your assumption that I would have taken advantage of a woman who was stoned to the point of passing out isn't very flattering, either," he went on.

"Stoned to the point of—" Megan croaked out. Stoned? He thought she'd been stoned? Of all the—

"Yeah," he confirmed laconically. "And, come to think of it, I'm not thrilled by the thought that if I *had* been degenerate enough to take advantage of you, you could *possibly* have forgotten the experience..." He emphasized this point by trailing one finger casually down the curve of her cheek. She felt the touch clear down to her toes.

Megan pulled back. "You—you think I was on drugs last night?" she exploded, deciding to let the monumental presumption of his last remark pass—at least for the moment. "You think that's why I can't remember what happened?"

Swann caught her chin, forcing her to meet his gaze. "Honey, you were dead to the world when I fished you out of the pool early this morning," he informed her trenchantly.

Megan swallowed.

"Pool?"

"That's right." Swann nodded, letting her chin go. "I lost track of you about midnight. As near as I can figure, you wandered outside. The caterers were cleaning up after everybody had left when all of a sudden you loomed out of nowhere by the cabana and—" He made a gesture indicating a dive. "Into the pool. They started shouting; I jumped in and dragged you out. From the way your pupils reacted when I checked those pretty hazel eyes of yours, I'd say you'd crash landed after a damned high flight." His eyes chilled to the color of surgical steel. "Funny, when I spotted you last night, I had you pegged as smart, not stupid."

If Megan had tried to chew over all the food for thought this particular string of remarks provided, she probably would have choked to death. Strangely, what she found hardest to swallow was Swann's frank admission that she had caught his interest the night before. Taking a deep breath, she decided to ignore this point.

Instead, she made up her mind to concentrate on refuting his basic misinterpretation of the previous night's events. Whatever those events *were*. His description of what had happened stirred only the dimmest of recollections.

"Look . . . Swann. Maybe I did go outside during the party. And maybe I did, um, fall into your pool—"

"Pass out into my pool."

"All right. All right! I passed out into your pool! But I do *not* do drugs. Do you understand?" She had too much respect for her mental and physical health—and, thanks to her father and to their shared profession, too much respect for the law—to indulge in illegal narcotics. "The only pills I take are allergy tablets, and the only reason I take them is that I don't want to spend my life sneezing and scratching hives."

"Allergy tablets?" His dark brows came together.

She nodded emphatically, pleased to have made an impression. "I don't even *drink* because of them," she added virtuously.

His reaction to this declaration was not what she'd expected. "Don't even drink *what?*" he questioned sharply.

"Alcohol!" she snapped irritably. What did he think she was talking about? Ovaltine?

Swann's sensually carved features went grim. "In that case, Megan, you're damned lucky you didn't wake up in some emergency ward getting your stomach pumped. Christ, you're lucky you woke up at all, considering the amount of liquor I saw you guzzling—"

It was the third time he'd made it clear that he'd had his eye on her the night before. Under different circumstances, she might have found this flattering. But now—

"I was drinking fruit punch," she contradicted flatly, tilting her chin challengingly. Her certainty about this point was based on two vivid memories. First, there was her recall of the punch itself. It wasn't easy to forget something that, while deliciously refreshing, had been a singularly vile shade of phosphorescent pink and garnished with slices of bright green kiwi fruit and a bobbing flotilla of maraschino cherries. Second, there was the indelible mental image of the man who had been ladling up the stuff. Megan had recognized him instantly: Albert "Boomer" Jankowski, Nightshade's drummer. His hair was an even deeper shade of red than her own, and he was huge, possessing the shambling charisma of a grizzly bear.

"That 'punch' was made from Boomer's Chloroform Cocktail recipe," Swann told her. "It's usually served in a lead-lined bowl."

"Chlor—but he said it was fruit juice!"

"Oh, it was. And, knowing Boomer, he probably stomped the fresh fruit with his bare feet to get the juice. But the recipe also calls for vodka and three or four different kinds of fruit brandy. Plus a couple of scoops of lemon sherbet, of course."

"Oh, of course," Megan agreed faintly, feeling her stomach turn over. Vodka, brandy . . . and lemon sherbet? Ye gods, Swann was right. She was lucky she hadn't ended up in some emergency ward. She'd had three—no, four—cups of the stuff.

"Are you all right, Megan?" he asked. Swann sounded genuinely concerned. He also shaped her name like a caress. "You look a little green."

"Yes . . . well, green is supposed to be one of my best colors," she returned with an attempt at a laugh.

"Seriously—"

"I'm okay," she assured him. "I guess—I guess it's no wonder that I passed out," she said after a few seconds, feeling extremely awkward. Lord, how could she have been so naive? How could she have believed that people would be serving plain fruit punch at a party for some of the most notorious members of the rock world? "And I suppose it's understandable that you thought what you thought . . . about the drugs. But I really don't—"

He silenced her by pressing two fingers gently against her mouth. "I'm sure you don't," he cut her off. "As I said, I had you pegged as smart, not stupid, and I usually have a pretty good eye for that sort of thing." Although he removed his hand, the feel of his touch lingered. "Now, I tell you what," he continued coolly, "why don't you get dressed and come downstairs? I'll fix us some coffee and we can sort all of this out."

"I—uh—" Whatever Megan had been about to say, it was driven right from her mind by Swann's nonchalantly getting out of bed.

For all her blushes, Megan Louise Harper wasn't an innocent. She wasn't a prude, either. She'd seen men wearing nothing but their underwear before. After all, she'd grown up in a household with two brothers. And she'd been married for five years.

What she *wasn't* used to was having a man she'd barely met flaunt his seminaked body in her face.

Not that this particular seminaked body didn't merit a little flaunting. Colin Swann had one of those lithe, lean, male physiques that could stand up to unashamed display from all angles in broad daylight. He was an inch or so over six feet tall. The muscle and sinew beneath his tanned skin was hard and sleek. Yet his physical power was tempered by a controlled grace that was evident even when he was completely still.

Hazel eyes met gray and Megan realized with a shock that Swann wasn't flaunting himself. He'd gotten out of bed in his current state of near-undress because it had been the natural thing to do. He was at ease with his body; it obviously surprised him that she wasn't that way, too.

Megan wasn't certain whether she should feel insulted or flattered.

"Sorry," Swann said with terse but apparent sincerity as he bent to retrieve a pair of black cord jeans from the floor. He donned the snug-fitting garment with smooth, economical movements. "I would have worn pajamas last night, but I don't own any."

Somehow, she found that very easy to believe.

"I—I didn't mean to stare," she said after a pause.

Swann zipped the fly of the jeans and snapped the waistband closed. The needle-wale corduroy hugged his pelvis and thighs like Saran Wrap. "There's no need for you to apologize. You're welcome to stare all you like." He raked his hand back through his dark, faintly wavy hair, revealing the widow's peak in the center of his hairline. The peak underscored his devilish good looks. "I'm used to it."

"But—"

"Besides," he continued, his silver-gray eyes running over her. "If the positions were reversed, I'd be staring at you."

Megan felt her cheeks catch fire again. Damn the man! He was enough to drive her to wearing a paper bag over her head—permanently! "I think I'll pass, thank you," she responded stiffly.

"Okay." He grinned. "I'll head downstairs and start the coffee. By the way, if you're wondering about your clothes, they're in there." He inclined his head toward a closed door. "The master bath. I'm afraid your stuff may not be in the best of shape thanks to your little belly flop. And your shoes and purse are missing."

"I understand." Megan remained silent for a moment or two, watching him pivot and walk toward the door, his stride long and easy. "Uh—Swann?" she blurted out as he reached the exit.

He paused and glanced back at her. "Yes?"

"I—" She hesitated, nibbling on her lower lip. Come on, Megan, she prompted herself. You've already asked the really embarrassing question about last night. This one should be simple. "Are you the one—did you undress me?'

He nodded. "You were soaking wet. It seemed like

the least I could do after I checked your pupils and your pulse."

"I see." Something—and Megan had no great desire to discover what—told her that Swann's method of checking a woman's pulse wasn't approved by the Red Cross. It was a good thing he wasn't checking her pulse now. It was pounding like a tom-tom.

"I was ready to administer artificial respiration, too, but you didn't need it."

"Oh." She hesitated, looking down at the purple shirt she wore. Lord, how am I going to write this up in my report? she wondered. Dad's such a stickler about ethical, professional behavior—he'll have a coronary!

"Megan?"

She glanced up. "Do you mind telling me why you put me in *your* bed?" She winced as the question came out. Swift, Megan Louise. Really swift. That's a classic setup line if there ever was one, she scolded herself.

Remarkably, Swann didn't take advantage of the opening although a blaze of repressed laughter turned his eyes to molten silver.

"I put you in my bed because it's the only one in the house," he answered simply. Then he smiled. "See you in a few minutes, Megan."

Megan found her clothes in the bathroom as promised. The scoop-necked, sleeveless, cream knit dress had dripped and dried into reasonable condition as had her underwear. But the cream and green jacket that completed the ensemble was a wrinkled mess. Rolling her eyes, she imagined what would happen if she put the cost of replacing it on her monthly expense account.

And, of course, there was the little matter of her missing shoes and purse . . .

Sighing, Megan surveyed her surroundings. The size of the master bath was enough to leave her speechless. It was larger than the living room of her apartment. Esther

Williams could have performed a water ballet in the huge sunken tub.

The decor was sybaritic in the extreme. There was lush, dove-gray carpeting, gleaming ebony ceramics, sleek silvery-toned marble, and what appeared to be an endless expanse of perfectly polished mirrors. Besides the usual array of bathroom accessories, there was a three-line telephone and a color television set. And the small, built-in refrigerator by the sink was stocked with vintage champagne and beluga caviar. Megan knew this because she opened it and checked.

Although Megan liked luxury as much as the next person, she couldn't help feeling vaguely disturbed—and strangely disappointed—by the unbridled hedonism the setting revealed. There was also something unnerving in being confronted by a seemingly infinite number of reflections of her leggy, five-foot-six-inch body.

She dressed quickly, wanting to obliterate the image. That done, she devoted a couple of futile minutes to trying to fingercomb her unruly curls into order.

Pretty was not an adjective she would apply to the milky-skinned, slightly angular face that gazed back at her from the mirrors. *Interesting* was closer to the mark, she felt. Her beauty, such as it was, was of a more sophisticated sort. Although her short, fluffy hairstyle and wide hazel eyes made her look younger than her actual age, a closer examination revealed intriguing signs of mature intelligence and passion—particularly in the set of her stubborn jaw and full mouth.

Megan frowned at her reflection as she abandoned her efforts to deal with her hair. Okay, so she didn't look her best this morning. She didn't look her worst, either, which was fairly amazing, considering what apparently had happened to her. She shuddered for a moment. All in all, she'd been very, very lucky.

Telling herself it was a matter of professional curiosity, Megan conducted a quick investigation of the upstairs before going down to join Swann. There were two other baths and three other generously proportioned rooms.

There were no other beds.

Shaking her head, Megan tried not to wonder about the implications of this as she came downstairs. She also tried not to speculate about what had happened to her shoes and purse.

Swann's new home was a beachfront house located in Malibu, California's ever-popular and extremely pricey enclave for show business celebrities and the artistically inclined. The staircase from the second floor led down to a huge, white stucco living room. Sandblasted beams and bleached oak floors emphasized the airy, casual atmosphere.

So did the absence of furniture, except for a few large pillows scattered about the floor. They were covered in an exquisite embroidered fabric that looked as though it had been purchased in some bazaar in Marrakesh.

No furniture. How was that possible? She distinctly remembered sitting on a long, contemporary leather sofa the night before. She also recalled a gleaming, state-of-the-art sound system set up and blaring.

Chewing the inside of her lip, Megan glanced out the sweeping expanse of glass doors to her right. The doors opened to a pool . . . *the* pool, she assumed. Beyond that was the Pacific Ocean. The view was beautiful. The clear, aquamarine water in the pool sparkled in the warm, June morning light. The Italian-tiled deck—enlivened here and there by tubs of green plants and pots of bright blossoms—was an open invitation to sun worshippers.

No wonder she'd gravitated out there the night before. Megan had a vague memory of how enticing the area had looked under the moonlight. Despite an unfortunate tendency toward sunburning, she'd always loved anything and everything connected with water and the outdoors. One of her college roommates, a biology major with an inexplicable faith in astrology, had told her that was because she was an Aquarius, one of the zodiac's water signs.

Forget the pool, Megan, she counseled herself firmly, turning away from the appealing vista. Forget everything about this place. *Especially* the man who owns it! Harper Security is just going to have to come up with somebody else for the "inside" part of this job. After last night, you definitely are *out!*

After a few false turns, Megan let her nose lead her to Swann and the promised cup of coffee. The kitchen she walked into was designed along the same spacious dimensions as the rest of the house. With its white-plastered walls, terra-cotta tiling, and ultramodern appliances, it was an attractive combination of the cozy and the contemporary. It also had a gorgeous view of the ocean.

"I think I found your purse," Swann announced as she came in. He pointed to a small, green lizard clutch bag on the counter next to him.

Megan retrieved it with a sense of relief. She snapped it open, doing a quick mental inventory.

"In case you're worried, I didn't check inside it," Swann told her.

Megan shut the bag and looked at him. "I didn't think you had," she said honestly. Though, in truth, it wouldn't have mattered much. Taking a cue from Kyle's advice about working undercover, she'd carefully removed all traces of her professional identity from her purse before setting out for last night's party.

Swann's dark brows went up. "Well, it's encouraging to know your opinion of me isn't totally negative." He extended a mug to her. "Coffee?" he inquired conversationally.

Megan felt herself flush. Murmuring a word of thanks, she took the mug. She gulped a healthy swallow of the dark, fragrant brew to cover her uneasiness.

"I'd offer you cream and sugar," Swann remarked

genially, leaning back against the counter with the in-
dolent grace of a jungle cat, "but the cupboards are bare
at the moment."

"I drink it black."

"Ah, a woman after my own heart."

"I'd imagine there are a lot of those," she said, giving
him a narrow glance. Daylight definitely liked him. Rather
than revealing the signs of rock-and-roll dissipation she'd
assumed must be in his face, the sunlight pouring into
the kitchen warmed the sculpted austerity of his handsome features, making him look younger . . . more ac-
cessible.

"My reputation precedes me, I take it," he said, apparently not offended by her sarcasm.

"Discretion doesn't seem to be your—ah—thing."

"Probably not," he conceded with a shrug. "But, in
the interests of accuracy, I'm forced to admit it's not
usually my heart women are after. My body and my
bankbook, yes. But my heart . . ."

Megan decided it was time to get off this topic.

"This may sound strange," she said after a moment,
"but I'd swear there was furniture down here last night."

"There was. The caterers brought it."

"You rented a houseful of furniture for one night?"
The extravagance of this astonished her almost as much
as the unabashed luxury of the bathroom had. Colin Swann
clearly indulged in a lifestyle she could barely imagine
. . . much less afford.

"I only rented furniture for the downstairs," he said.
"It's tax deductible and it's not as expensive as it sounds.
In any case, I had to have something for people to sit
on, didn't I? I had planned to have this place put together
before last night's little bash, but I haven't had time to
pick out what I need."

"*You're* decorating the house?"

He grinned. "You think the only thing a rock musician
knows about furniture is how to trash it?"

"No. Of course not," she denied quickly. "I just—I assumed you'd have—well a—decorator."

"Oh, I had a decorator." Swann smiled. His name was Waldo Vandergloss. My mother recommended him."

"Had?" Megan didn't need to ask why Swann had turned to his mother for advice about decorating. Alexandra Collins—semiretired silver screen queen, adored wife of producer-director Sir Richard Swann, and Hollywood hostess *extraordinaire*—was celebrated for her trendsetting tastes.

"I fired him after I got a look at the master bathroom."

"Oh. Well—it's a very—ah—*striking* room."

"The price tag was fairly striking, too," he stated. "Still, I'm hoping to recoup part of the cost. A buddy of mine is doing a music video involving the decline and fall of the Roman Empire. He wants to rent the bathroom for a location shoot."

Megan had to smile. "Actually, it reminded me of something out of the Last Days of Pompeii."

Swann smiled at this. "Everything but a volcano," he said. "Waldo probably would have installed one of those, too, if I hadn't given him the boot. The thousand bucks' worth of caviar in the refrigerator was the last straw. The last time I ate caviar I was eight. I took some off the buffet at one of my mother's parties. It was the most awful stuff I ever tasted. I've had no desire to follow up the experience."

Megan laughed. "Was Waldo Vandergloss upset when you fired him?" she asked.

"Not at all. He took the job out of fear of offending my mother. She's one of his best clients. Clearly he considered the assignment slumming. Waldo doesn't 'do' the beach, you see. He may be allergic to sand."

"Well, if nothing else, you have a phone in your bathroom. I always thought that would be the ultimate convenience."

"It's the ultimate something," he said, his mouth twisting. "Incidentally, that reminds me—is there anybody you'd like to call?"

"Call?" she repeated, startled. She was going to have to touch base with her father, of course, but there was no way Swann could know that. And there certainly was no way she was going to tell him!

"Yes. There must be someone wondering where you were all night."

Megan blinked, suddenly realizing what he really wanted to know. It seemed to her he was raising the issue a bit late. "Don't you think you should have asked what you're asking before?" she inquired pointedly.

"You mean—" He glanced upward.

"Yes."

"Probably," he conceded. "Seeing that I didn't, will you at least give me a hint about whether some irate husband or lover is like to come gunning for me because you happened to mix alcohol with allergy tablets and end up in my bed?"

His choice of words sent an unpleasant shiver snaking through her. "No irate husband," she said flatly, trying to quell her sudden sense of unease. Somebody might very well be gunning for Colin Swann. That's why Harper Security had been called in. "I'm divorced."

"What about jealous lovers?"

She frowned, glancing away for a moment. "You don't have to worry about that, either." Despite the encouragement of her family, Megan had scarcely dated since the breakup of her marriage to Doug. It had taken her a long time to recover from the hurtful discovery of her ex-husband's infidelities and the trauma of the divorce.

"I see." Swann studied her with unnerving intensity for several moments. "What about the guy who brought you to the party last night?"

Megan hesitated. They were getting into touchy territory. Kyle had told her that improvisation was an important part of undercover work; she decided that whatever she improvised at this point had better be as close to the truth as possible. "The 'guy' who brought me last night was your manager," she said. The same 'guy,' she added mentally, who's hired my father's security agency to protect you!

"Bernie?" Swann looked surprised. "Bernie McGillis?"

"Yes."

"You really came with—" He broke off, his eyes narrowing. "Wait a minute. You said your name is Megan. Not Megan . . . Howard?"

"Harper," she corrected, feeling a new sense of uneasiness.

"Harper," he repeated. "Megan Harper." He started to laugh. "I don't believe this," he said finally.

"What don't you believe?" she asked suspiciously.

"You're the woman Bernie wants me to hire as my son's new nanny!"

CHAPTER TWO

"So," BERNIE McGILLIS announced with a satisfied nod about five hours later, "everything's settled." Folding his hands on the top of his incredibly cluttered desk, Swann's manager let his gaze move from Megan, to her brother Kyle, to her father, Simon. Bernie was in his middle fifties. He was of middling height, middling paunchiness, and middling baldness. *Wrinkled* and *rumpled* seemed to be key words in his concept of fashion—if a man who wore an unraveling, acid-green polyester knit tie could be said to have a concept of fashion.

In all, Bernie McGillis was fairly unprepossessing— except for his eyes. One look at the go-for-the-jugular shrewdness they contained and Megan had decided that this was not a man to underestimate.

Megan put a lot of stock in what she saw in other people's eyes. Experience had taught her that there was a great deal of truth to the saying that eyes were the windows to a person's soul. Hadn't she known that her

21

five-year marriage to Doug was irretrievably over because of what she'd seen in his eyes the night she'd finally confronted him with the evidence of his infidelities? He'd tried to lie his way out of it with kisses as well as words. But his eyes had given him away.

Perhaps, she thought with a sudden flash of insight, that was one of the reasons she'd found Colin Swann so unnerving. It went beyond his celebrity, his sexuality, and the situation she'd found herself in with him. No, his *eyes* had disturbed her. They were more mirrors than windows. Despite their expressiveness, the essence of their silver-gray depths was an enigma.

"We worked out a deal with Swann's limousine company," Kyle was saying with the take-charge confidence that was so much a part of him. Two years younger than Megan, he was as tough and resourceful as he was good-looking. Kyle Harper was very much a man's man; he was also something of a lady killer. Megan hadn't missed his starting a promising flirtation with Bernie McGillis's curvy, starlet-pretty secretary. "I've gone through a defensive driving course, so I'll be filling in for the regular chauffeur. We'll be slipping people in around Swann the way you've outlined, too. Very casual. Very offhand. He won't notice a thing. And, of course, we'll have Megan on the inside as our ace in the hole."

"It seems to me our 'ace in the hole,' hasn't said very much," Simon Harper said suddenly, his rumbling voice thoughtful. Megan's father was a bulky bulldog of a man. He'd started Harper Security twenty years before, after he was disabled in the line of duty as a Los Angeles police officer and was forced to retire. He'd been wheelchair-bound for two decades. He was a man of bedrock integrity and iron will.

Megan flushed, feeling three pairs of eyes fix on her. Her father wasn't a man who talked a lot, but when he did speak, he made it count. Megan had given her father and brother an extremely sanitized—all right, a virtually fabricated—account of her experiences at Colin Swann's housewarming. She'd done so expecting to hear from Bernie McGillis that his client had decided she was not the kind of woman to take care of his son. But no. The first thing the manager had said after greeting them in his waiting room was that Swann had just called to say Megan Harper was precisely the type of nanny he was looking for.

Now she was stuck with the lie. Her only hope for getting out of this job—and, after what had happened, she certainly didn't want any further involvement with Colin Swann, did she?—was that young P.J. Swann would take an instant dislike to her.

"Meg?" her father prompted. Something about his tone made her wonder how convincing her account of the previous night's events had been.

"I—I guess it's that I'm still a little . . . well, I know a lot about bodyguarding and security field work in theory, but I haven't had much practical experience," she said finally. "And this whole thing is so—so strange."

"Starting with these damn threatening letters Swann's been getting." Bernie McGillis nodded. There was an expression lurking in his eyes Megan couldn't quite get a fix on. It made her ask herself what else Swann might have said when he'd telephoned. "If we can just figure out who's sending them and *why*—" He frowned. "I don't have to tell you people that celebrities like Swann attract nuts. Maybe this . . . correspondent is some harmless crank letting off a little steam. I hope to hell that's all it is. But, as I said when I first contacted you, I've got a bad gut feeling about it."

"I go along with that," Simon Harper said. "The tone of these letters has become progressively more sinister over the past two months. And the threats are getting more specific. It's almost as though whoever's sending them is working himself up to *do* something. And although our graphologist's analysis of the handwriting didn't give us much, she did say there were definite signs of emotional disturbance."

"Are you having doubts about handling this, Megan?" Kyle asked. "I'm not trying to put you down—I mean, your background with kids makes you the perfect candidate for an undercover nanny. But you really haven't had much honest-to-God experience in bodyguarding."

"I just wish this didn't have to be so underhanded," Megan cut in. "It's bad enough not knowing who we're up against in terms of these letters, but we can't let Swann know what we're up to either—"

"Hey, I can understand your being uptight about that," Bernie interrupted. "And, believe me, I don't like the idea of deceiving Swann anymore than you do. Less, probably. Because I know him and I know how he feels about people who lie to him. Hell, he'll probably nail my hide to the wall if he finds out what I've done. But, dammit, it's for his own good."

"What—what about his son?" Megan asked, deciding to follow up on one point that had been troubling her. "If he cares for his child as much as you've said—"

"Swann is crazy about P.J. But the kid's security hasn't been an issue up until now. He's been living with his grandparents for the past three months, ever since his last nanny left."

"From what Steve says, Alexandra Collins and Sir Richard Swann have one of the best security systems in Hollywood," Kyle commented. The Steve he referred to was his and Megan's elder brother, and the agency's electronic genius. Recently he'd been out of town, on a long-term case. He'd only just returned.

"Yeah," Bernie said. "They've supposedly got gadgets the C.I.A. doesn't have yet." He turned back to Megan. "Look, trust me, Megan—I can call you Megan, can't I?—*trust me*. I've tried to use P.J. to drum a little sense into Swann's stubborn skull, but it hasn't worked. Swann's told me *he'll* take care of his son—whatever that means."

"But I still don't understand why he won't take normal security precautions for himself," Megan said. "He must realize—"

"I know, I know," the manager cut in with a trace of weariness. "If somebody else was mentioned in these letters, you can bet Swann would see they were protected. But as long as he's the only target—no go. And don't ask me to explain. I can't. That's just the way he is. Maybe his mother introduced him to John Wayne when he was a kid and he got a heavy dose of the cowboy code. Maybe it's tied up with his father. The Swann family supposedly traces back to King Arthur and the Round Table. Then again, Swann spent a couple of years in Japan when he was in his early twenties. Could be he decided to become a secret samurai. Anything's possible."

"I can see where he's coming from," Kyle observed in a tone that was clearly tinged with admiration.

"As long as he's the only one directly in danger, he wants to handle it on his own terms," Megan said softly, almost to herself. Cowboy. Knight. Samurai. Odd, how easily she could envision Swann in any of those roles.

"Exactly," Bernie confirmed emphatically. "He puts up with security people when he's out on tour. But it's no way, José, as far as having them in his private life."

"I suppose that kidnapping episode when he was young might have something to do with it," Simon Harper commented.

For a moment, the manager looked a little surprised. Then he nodded. "That's right, you were with the L.A.P.D. back then, weren't you?"

"What are you talking about?" Megan asked, puzzled.

"Well, with a movie star mother and a movie mogul father, you can imagine Swann had a pretty public childhood," Bernie explained. "It wasn't one of those 'Mommie Dearest' routines, but it wasn't ordinary, either. Anyway, there were kidnapping threats—plus one nearly successful attempt when he was nine or ten. Alexandra got very paranoid and hired a platoon of security people. I don't know all the details, but I gather Swann had bodyguards trailing around after him—or trying to trail around after him—until he graduated from high school."

Kyle whistled. "Anybody'd have a hang-up about bodyguards after something like that."

Megan had to agree.

"So—" Bernie said, glancing at Megan's father and younger brother before locking his sharp eyes on her once again. "Megan will go to meet P.J. tomorrow afternoon at Lady Swann's place in Beverly Hills. If that works out the way I think it will—the kid's a real sweetheart, believe me—we're all set."

The question is, Megan thought, all set for what?

Ten minutes later, the three Harpers were waiting for the elevator to take them down to the lobby of the building where Bernie McGillis's office was located. As the car arrived, Megan launched into what she hoped was a convincing imitation of a person who'd just remembered something important.

"Oh, I forgot to find out what time I'm supposed to meet P.J.," she said.

"Call McGillis when we get back to the office," Kyle suggested, stepping into the empty car and hitting the OPEN button so the doors wouldn't slide shut while their father maneuvered his wheelchair in.

"No," she demurred quickly. "I think I'll firm it up now. You two don't have to wait; I've got my own car." She had a bone she wanted to pick with Bernie McGillis—alone.

"We'll see you at the office, then, Meg," her father said.

Bernie McGillis didn't seem at all surprised by Megan's solo return. "I thought you might come back," he commented.

"Did you?" Megan countered, crossing to stand in front of his desk. The general untidiness of his office was in keeping with his unkempt appearance. She wondered fleetingly how he could find anything in the confusion of legal documents, album covers, posters, PR releases, and old newspapers and magazines.

"Yeah. Your reservations about this job wouldn't have anything to do with Swann finding a pair of size seven-and-a-half double-A sandals in the deep end of his pool, would they?"

If Megan had been a target, the manager would have just nailed her for a bull's-eye. She felt her cheeks go beet red. "Sandals?" she asked, mustering all the dignity she could. Damn! She'd insisted Swann call a taxi for her. Getting in it in her bare feet had been bad enough. She didn't want to contend with his manager's embarrassing conjectures as well.

"Swann mentioned them when he called. He seemed to think they might be yours."

A candidate for canonization couldn't have worn a more innocent expression than the one beaming from Bernie's face at this point. Megan knew enough about human nature to recognize she was being maneuvered by a master.

"You know, Mr. McGillis," she began to say after a few seconds, "you left me in a very awkward posi— situation last night." Megan's father was a master at maneuvering people, too, and one of the things she'd learned from him was that it helped to put the *other* person on the defensive.

"I did?"

"Yes. You brought me to Swann's housewarming party to—how did you put it?—scope things out. Then you deserted me—"

"Deserted? Hey, hold on. I checked all over for you last night after I got ready to leave. When I couldn't find you, I figured you'd met somebody—you know. You're

unattached, gorgeous—hell, you didn't exactly pass un-
noticed."

Megan gnawed her lower lip, trying to decide whether
this last remark was a veiled reference to Swann's watching her at the party. "Look, in point of fact," she said
with flat precision, "while you were supposedly checking
for me, I apparently was wandering around outside. I—
um—I'd drunk some of Boomer's Chloroform Cocktail
mix without knowing it had alcohol in it. I take allergy
pills and I had a reaction—"

"You passed out?" The inquiry was shrewd.

"Into the pool!"

"Hmm." Bernie accepted this revelation calmly. "I
take it you haven't told your . . . family about this?"

Megan stiffened, her temper starting to flare. "I woke
up this morning in Colin Swann's bed wearing nothing
but a Nightshade T-shirt!" How could she have told her
father or Kyle that?

"Yeah, I saw the way Swann was watching you,"
Bernie said reflectively. "But, hey, I wouldn't let one
night worry you. If you're P.J.'s nanny, that sort of thing
won't happen—"

"Nothing happened!"

There was an uncomfortable silence. Megan realized
she'd come humiliatingly close to stamping her foot to
underscore her assertion.

She took a steadying breath. "I don't think I'm the
right person for this job," she said, her voice quiet but
determined.

Bernie sighed. "I do. I think you're the right person
for both jobs: taking care of P.J. *and* protecting Swann
from the inside. Your father obviously thinks so too, and
he's a man whose judgment I'd certainly trust in this kind
of situation." With the infallible timing of a master ne-
gotiator, he paused, judiciously letting Megan stew in
her own juices for nearly thirty seconds before going on.
"Look, go meet the kid tomorrow. Afterward, if you still

have these reservations — well, it's your call." He smiled. "If nothing else, you'll get those sandals of yours back. Right?"

Swann's parents lived in an exquisite Georgian mansion. The immaculately manicured grounds surrounding it would have made the head greenskeeper at the world's poshest country club weep with envy. It was the kind of place that was grand yet gracious, that exuded money and taste without being ostentatious.

"Miss Harper?" the butler who answered the door inquired in a British accent so plummy it could have been spread on bread. His eyes flickered over her, cataloguing her from the tips of her curly red-gold hair to the toes of her sensible navy pumps.

"That's right," Megan confirmed, straightening her shoulders and lifting her chin. She had the feeling that the grave major-domo had just priced her trim navy skirt and crisp white cotton blouse to the penny. She also had the feeling that the cost of her entire outfit was substantially less than the lady of the house spent per week on pedicures.

"Excellent," the man intoned. "This way. Her ladyship is waiting."

Her ladyship. Megan had forgotten that Alexandra Collins used her husband's name — and title — in private life. What did that mean? Was she supposed to curtsy when introduced? Or maybe she was supposed to kiss the twenty-carat sapphire-and-diamond engagement ring Swann's mother reportedly never took off?

Moving with a stately tread, the butler led Megan through the house. If the lavish decor were an accurate reflection of Waldo Vandergloss's style, Megan could understand why he had disdained working on Swann's beach house.

She barely controlled a smile as she speculated on what the master bathroom of *this* place looked like.

The butler escorted her to a terrace that overlooked a statuary-surrounded swimming pool. There were two people in the pool. One was a dark-haired little boy standing in the shallow end and splashing with puppylike abandon. The other was a tall, tanned man with water-sleeked black hair who balanced, motionless, on the diving board at the far end of the pool.

Although he was a good fifty yards away and had his back to her, Megan recognized Colin Swann instantly. Her heart gave a curious lurch as she watched him launch himself effortlessly into a perfect flip.

"Miss Harper, m'lady," the butler announced, making a small bow. Then he turned and went back into the mansion.

Alexandra Collins—Lady Swann—had been sitting in the shade of an umbrella when the butler spoke. She rose with the deliberate grace of a woman accustomed to having her every movement scrutinized by cameras.

"Miss Harper," she said warmly, extending one pale, beautifully manicured hand. "How nice to meet you." Her melodious voice was, in its own way, as distinctive as her son's.

"Lady Swann," Megan responded, shaking the proffered hand. Alexandra Collins's firm grip belied her drawing room languor.

Swann's mother was in her late fifties. Petite, slender, and delicately featured, she wore her age lightly. True, there were wrinkles on her throat, around her mouth, and at the corners of her blue eyes. Her fair hair held a great deal of silver, too. But her overall aura was one of youthful vitality tempered by mature serenity.

"Please sit down," she invited with a lovely smile, surveying Megan with unabashed interest. "The boys should be out of the pool in a few minutes."

"Thank you," Megan said, taking the seat the other woman waved her to. Despite her best efforts, she couldn't keep from glancing toward "the boys." Swann had moved to the shallow end of the pool. He was standing in the water like a pagan sea god while his son bobbed around him like a cork.

Suddenly, P.J. stopped horsing around and pointed a dripping finger toward the terrace. Before Megan had a chance to avert her gaze, Swann turned. Their eyes met and clung for the space of a heartbeat, obliterating the distance between them.

The tug of attraction she experienced shook her. She'd spent the better part of the past twenty-four hours trying to convince herself that the powerful feelings Swann had stirred in her the day before had been an aberration. She'd told herself over and over again that she hadn't been responsible for what had happened. How could she have been? Her synapses had been scrambled by the combination of her allergy tablets and Boomer Jankowski's potently alcoholic Chloroform Cocktail mix.

It did nothing for her peace of mind to discover that her synapses were still decidedly scrambled.

Swann may be the one who's being threatened, Megan thought uncomfortably. But *I'm* the one who needs protection.

"—rather contradictory," Alexandra Collins was saying. "I hope you understand."

Megan started. "I'm sorry," she apologized, turning her attention to Swann's mother. "I didn't hear what you were saying."

Nice going, Megan Louise, she chided herself. Where's your professional pride? If you're going to go through with this charade, at least make an effort to maintain your cover! A prospective nanny does *not* tune out the mother of her potential employer during a job interview!

Surprisingly, the older woman didn't take offense. Instead, her blue eyes flicked briefly toward the pool and then returned to focus on Megan's slightly flushed face. Megan had the feeling she was ticking something off a mental check list.

"The view can be rather distracting," Alexandra observed blandly. "What I was saying is that I have decidedly mixed feelings about my son's hiring you—or anyone else—to look after P.J. You see, my grandson's been staying here since his last nanny, Mrs. Lynton, left. Now, I understand that Colin has to get around to replacing her. But once he does—well, I'm very much the doting grandmother. And I'll miss P.J. dreadfully when he leaves, especially since my husband is away on location."

"Of course." Megan nodded her understanding.

Alexandra picked a minuscule bit of lint off her ivory linen pants. The elegant movement of her hand made her famous diamond-and-sapphire engagement ring shoot white and blue fire. "I must say, you *do* come highly recommended by Bernie McGillis," she remarked thoughtfully. "And Colin seems quite . . . impressed by you, too."

"I'm glad to hear that," Megan said, adopting what she hoped was a properly appreciative air. At the same time, she wondered just exactly what she should make of the pause in Alexandra's last comment. Swann's mother was an accomplished actress. She didn't just throw in pauses for no reason. It had to mean something. But what?

"Of course, I have to admit you're younger and far more . . . attractive than I envisioned. I was expecting—"

"You were expecting a leggy, strawberry-blonde who blushes," Colin Swann's distinctive voice cut in lazily. "Because that's how I described Megan to you. You were *hoping* for Mary Poppins."

Megan turned, feeling herself go pink. Swann was standing at the top of the stone stairs that led from the terrace to the pool. His thick dark hair was slicked back from his forehead to reveal his widow's peak. He flashed a provocative grin at Megan; his even teeth gleamed whiter than the towel he had slung around his neck. He wore nothing but an extremely brief pair of black swimming trunks. They rode low on his lean hips and stretched tight across his flat belly.

"Colin, dear, I do wish you'd stop sneaking up on me," his mother complained in a wonderfully grande-dame manner. "I'm tempted to tie a bell on you. And as for the other—you have no idea what I was hoping for. I certainly wasn't finding fault with Miss Harper for being young and beautiful. Quite the contrary." She punctuated this statement by bestowing a dazzling smile on Megan. The smile—unless Megan's ability to read other people's expressions had suddenly gone haywire—held more than a hint of feminine conspiracy.

But why would Alexandra Collins be conspiring with—Unless . . . good Lord! Could *she* be involved in Bernie McGillis's scheme for protecting her son, too?

"You should be aware that contrariness is one of my mother's favorite ploys, Megan," Swann said, crossing from the stairs with the lithe grace that seemed such a part of him. He dropped a kiss on Alexandra's cheek before sprawling comfortably in the chair next to Megan. There were only a few inches between his naked leg and her stockinged one.

"I think Miss Harper should be made aware of *your* favorite ploys," his mother countered tartly. Despite the lightly edged banter, the affection between the two was palpable.

"Oh, she's already been exposed to one or two of those. Haven't you, Megan?"

The teasing glint in his compelling eyes was enough to undermine Megan's good intentions. If Swann wasn't going to treat her like a proper nanny, she damned well wasn't going to behave like one!

"*Exposed* is just the right word, Mr. Swann," she agreed with sweet sarcasm, thinking of both the sight of his barely clad body climbing out of the bed they'd shared and his undressing her while she was unconscious.

Alexandra Collins cleared her throat delicately, her blue eyes darting back and forth as though she were watching a fascinating tennis match. "I believe Bernie McGillis said you have a degree in child psychology, Miss Harper?"

"Ah—child development," Megan said, thankful that she could be honest about at least some of her credentials. "I've done some work toward an M. A. in child psych."

"And you worked for a child care center before you became a nanny?"

"Yes." Megan had landed the child care job right out of college, thanks to an intern program she'd been involved in. Unfortunately, the center's funding had run out after several years. Unemployed, she'd agreed to take on some temporary work—ironically involving a kidnapping threat against the young daughter of a wealthy industrialist—at her father's agency. One thing had led to another, and she'd stayed on with Harper Security. Eventually, she'd met and married Doug Carlyle, a lawyer who'd hired the agency on behalf of a client.

"Why did you decide to become a nanny?" Swann asked curiously. "It seems an unusual occupation."

"I love children," Megan replied truthfully. "I've always wanted to work with them. I was often frustrated at the child care center because there were so many children and so little time to treat them as individuals. Being a nanny—I like one-on-one relationships."

She paused, swiftly reviewing the doctored part of her résumé in her head. Although Bernie McGillis had assured her that Swann would accept his word that her background had been thoroughly checked out, she knew she couldn't afford a slip. Even if she decided not to get involved in this case, she didn't want to make Swann suspicious about what his manager might be up to.

"My marriage broke up about a year ago," she went on. There was a murmur of sympathetic understanding from Alexandra Collins. "Since then, I've been looking after a number of different children." That was partially true. She *had* baby-sat for her brother Steve's three boys on a number of occasions. "But now I want something more permanent."

"Permanence is what *I* want for P.J.," Swann said. "I—"

"Speaking of P.J.—" Alexandra interrupted, looking toward the small figure climbing the ladder from the pool. "Darling," she said, beckoning. "Come and meet Miss Harper."

Megan turned. According to the information provided by Bernie McGillis, Peter Jordan Swann, now dripping wet, was exactly six years old. He was of average height and weight. His left knee was scraped and he had a Band-Aid on his right elbow. His dark, wet hair was the same color as his father's, but there was no real facial resemblance between the two. Colin Swann looked like a dangerously charming devil; P.J.'s features had been cast in a mischievously cherubic mold.

P.J. advanced across the patio. After carefully wiping his right hand dry on the towel he had draped around his neck in an obvious attempt to imitate his father's casual panache, he stuck it out at Megan. His manner was quite poised.

"Hi, Miss Harper." He examined her with bright eyes.

"Hi, P.J.," Megan responded, shaking his small hand.

"Are you the lady who fell in Daddy's pool?" he asked with an air of lively interest.

"I—" Megan shot Swann a sharp look. He gazed back at her steadily, a faint smile curling one corner of his sensual mouth.

"Are you?" P.J. pressed.

"Ah—yes," she confirmed. Out of the corner of her

eye, she saw Alexandra's brows lift delicately.

The little boy seemed pleased. "You lost your shoes, huh? Don't worry. Daddy's got them in a Baggie. Only they're really wrecked." He paused, scratching his snub nose. "Do you know Boomer? Daddy's drummer?"

Megan glanced at Swann again. The faint smile had grown to full-scale. "Yes," she said cautiously, "I've met Boomer."

"Well, he fell into a pool once, too. I helped push him. It was great. He made this really big splash." Giggling, P.J. illustrated his story with a hand motion and sound effects. Megan recognized the gesture as the one Swann had used the day before when relating what had happened to her. "It was like a tidal wave!" the youngster concluded exuberantly.

"P.J.," Swann said with a very parental mixture of amusement and exasperation. "Miss Harper hasn't agreed to come take care of you yet. I don't think you should be telling her how you push people into pools."

P.J. looked at his father. "But you did it, too!"

Megan had to fight to keep her face straight.

"P.J.—"

"Hey!" The little boy turned his wide blue-gray eyes back on Megan. "Daddy didn't *throw* you in his pool, did he?"

"*P.J.!*"

The child sighed. "Yes, Daddy?" he asked patiently.

"Remember that talk we had once about nosy questions?"

P.J. seemed to be thinking. "You mean that one where you said you'd answer anything I wanted to know only I should wait until it's a 'propriate time to ask?" he said finally.

"That's the one, buddy."

"But Miss Harper didn't get mad. Not like that other lady," the little boy argued. He glanced entreatingly at

Megan. "You *aren't* mad, are you?" he asked. "See, Daddy—she's laughing!"

It was true. Megan had lost her battle to keep from smiling. Despite all the other dynamics involved in this interview, she was too human not to relish the sight of Colin Swann, international rock star, being put on the spot by his six-year-old son.

Alexandra Collins was obviously taking some pleasure from the situation, too, because she suddenly spoke up.

"What 'other lady,' P.J.?" she inquired.

The little boy shrugged. "Just this lady who came out of Daddy's room at Mallory's," he replied indifferently. "Mallory's Daddy's friend," he explained to Megan. "We rented her house for a while. She used to be Molly V."

"The lead singer of Fallen Angel?" Megan questioned. She vaguely remembered seeing a picture of Swann singing alongside the glamorously sexy young woman, with her cloud-drift of dark hair.

"Yeah. Only she quit to get married. So Boomer, Coney, and Rick—they were in Fallen Angel, see— formed Nightshade with Daddy." He frowned. "Do you like rock-and-roll?"

Megan nodded. Although she was not about to admit it in front of Swann, she was a fervent Nightshade fan.

"Phew." P.J. grinned disarmingly. "Mrs. Lynton—she took care of me before—used to wear earplugs when we went to hear Daddy rehearse. She said his music was as—as—athletically offensive."

Swann gave a snort of laughter. "I think you mean aesthetically offensive, Peej."

"Oh, yeah. That was it," the little boy agreed. "Mrs. Lynton was weird about Daddy. Maybe because she was old. Like when the lady came out of Daddy's room—"

"Now, this was a lady who Mrs. Lynton saw coming out of your father's room?" Alexandra Collins questioned dulcetly. "I'm beginning to understand why she decided to leave, Colin," she added in a sparkling aside.

"Mother—"

"It's okay, Daddy," P.J. said with innocent assurance. "Mrs. Lynton didn't *see* the lady, Grandma Sandra. It was still early. She was still snoring and her hair was in pink rollers. I told her about it after she got up." Giggles bubbled out of him like carbonation in a soft drink. "She turned bright red. Like Miss Harper." He looked at Megan, his expression becoming serious. "Only *you* look pretty when your face turns red, Miss Harper," he declared with artless sincerity.

The conversational spotlight bounced back to Megan who, predictably, started to turn red again. "Ah, thank you, P.J.," she managed to say.

"Daddy likes pretty ladies," P.J. confided. "Sometimes, he even—"

"Put a cork in it, P.J.," Swann ordered quietly.

It was the voice of authority. It said a lot about Swann's relationship with his son that the little boy obeyed without balking.

"Okay," P.J. said. "Sorry, Daddy. Sorry, Miss Harper. Sorry, Grandma Sandra," he added for good measure. His grandmother waved her hand, trying to turn what sounded like a laugh into a convincing cough.

"It's all right, P.J.," Megan said. She wasn't feeling very charitable toward Swann at the moment, but she didn't want the child to think her irritation was directed at him.

The little boy gazed at her hopefully. "Do you—uh— like animals?" he questioned, changing the subject with an abruptness Megan knew to be typical of young children.

She smiled. "Yes, as a matter of fact, I do. I had a lot of pets when I was growing up." She supposed, looking back, that those pets had been early evidence of the nurturing instinct that seemed to be so strong in her. Other young girls might have been satisfied to pretend with dolls; she'd always wanted living things to cuddle and care for.

"You did?" P.J.'s face blossomed into a smile. "What kinds of pets?"

"Hmm—" She thought back fondly. "Well, I had a whole tankful of goldfish and guppies. And a rabbit named Bugs. And a cat I called Trouble because that was what he used to get me into when he caught mice and brought them to my mother—"

"Oh, *wow!*"

Megan laughed. "I had a couple of hamsters, too. And my brother had snakes and a monkey—"

"A monkey! A real *monkey?*"

Megan nodded. "We only had him for a little while, though. My father decided the monkey needed more space, so we gave him to a professor who could give him a good home."

"Boy, I'd like to have a monkey for even five minutes!"

"Do you have any pets?" Megan asked, touched by the little boy's enthusiasm. P.J. Swann was an endearingly natural child. And however many other things she might fault his father about, she sensed it was Swann who was making certain his son didn't turn into a spoiled brat.

"I have my gerbil Godzilla. He comes from Mongolia."

"Mongolia, hmm?"

"Well—" P.J. gave her a confiding smile and then glanced at his father. "Not *really* Mongolia. But, a long, long time ago, that's where gerbils started out. Daddy read me this book about them. See, I think maybe I want to be a vetinarian, so Daddy said I should start learning stuff now."

"That sounds like a very good idea," Megan said. Her eyes sought Swann's for a moment. The look that passed between them was warm with an unexpected but very intimate understanding.

"Anyway," P.J. continued, recalling her attention, "Godzilla's my only pet. But now that we have our own house, Daddy says maybe I can get a puppy." His mouth formed an O. "Hey! Since you know a lot about pets, you can help me pick it! I mean—" He faltered slightly. "I mean, *if* you decide to be my nanny. Do you think you will? It'd be fun, Miss Harper. I'll be good. Well, pretty good most of the time," he amended with scrupulous honesty. He darted another quick glance at his father. "And Daddy will promise to be good, too, if you'll come and live with us."

There was a pause. A decidedly pregnant pause.

Alexandra, who'd been silent throughout the whole exchange about pets, was the one to end it. "P.J., darling," she said brightly, "why don't you go in and ask Maria for some cookies?"

"But I don't want any—"

"You've had your chance to help with Miss Harper's interview," his grandmother cut in firmly. "Now she and your father have some things to discuss."

P.J. scratched his nose. "Okay," he said with obvious reluctance. Then he gave Megan a quick grin. "See you later, Miss Harper," he said, stressing the words as though just saying them carefully enough would make them come true. Without waiting for a response, he turned and ran to the house.

There was another pause. It was as tense, if not more, than the one that had preceded it.

"You've made a conquest of my son," Swann observed quietly. His voice seemed to twine around Megan's nerves like caressing tendrils.

"He's a wonderful little boy," she replied, meeting his silver-gray eyes as steadily as she could. It was plain that he was going to offer her the job. It was equally plain that she was going to take it.

He did offer it, but hardly in the words she expected.

"So, Miss Harper," he drawled slowly, "if I promise to be good, will you come and live with us?"

CHAPTER THREE

TWO WEEKS LATER, Megan stood in the living room of Swann's beach house. Methodically she tightened screws on the mechanism that locked the sliding glass doors that led to the pool, her brows drawn together into a frown of concentration.

Behind her, the once-empty living room was, like the rest of the place, completely and comfortably furnished. Somehow, in the four days following the housewarming party, Swann had arranged for a total decorating job. When Megan had expressed her astonishment at how quickly everything was done, he'd simply shrugged and said something about having had help from Patti Guarino. Patti was the wife of Nightshade's keyboard man, Coney. Swann had also made a grinning reference to cash and carry.

"Too bad somebody didn't spend a little more cash on this lock," Megan muttered to herself. Oh, it was perfectly adequate—as effective as any of the others in the house. But it was hardly foolproof. Any moderately skilled, reasonably determined burglar could open it in a matter of minutes.

She clicked her tongue while grappling with the unpleasant conviction that any *un*skilled and *un*reasonably determined person could smash through the double-glazed glass doors in a matter of seconds.

Unreasonable. *Irrational.* Swann had received another threatening letter the day before, or so Bernie McGillis had informed Harper Security. The manager's office screened all Swann's mail. This latest letter, postmarked Chicago, was like the previous ones. It was scribbled in black Magic Marker on cheap paper. Its message read in part: "I'm coming for you. I know what you did. You'll pay, Swann." It concluded—and this was new—"You never loved her."

There was no clue as to who "her" was. Given what she'd read about Swann's private life, Megan suspected the list of possibilities was lengthy.

Megan shivered a little and then gave the screw she was working on another partial turn. At least the beach house was wired with an alarm system. She'd discreetly checked that out shortly after she'd moved in. Again, the alarm system was perfectly adequate, but hardly state-of-the-art.

No, state-of-the-art security involved infrared cameras, electronic beams, heat sensors, and sound-activated equipment—the sorts of things her older brother, Steve, specialized in.

Megan glanced out the glass doors, letting her eyes sweep over the oceanside vista. The only person she could see was a burly man in a nondescript sweatsuit. He was plodding up and down the beach. He looked vaguely familiar. She squinted against the sun, trying to make out the details of his appearance and wondering where she might have seen him before.

There was something . . . out-of-place about the man.

Maybe it was the singularly joyless way he exercised. It looked as though he were trying to stomp the sand into submission. Or maybe it was his size that seemed odd. He certainly wasn't built like the typical beach athlete. Watching him jog was like watching a bulldozer trying to perform *Swan Lake*.

Don't let your imagination get out of hand, Megan Louise, she warned herself. This section of Malibu has its own private security patrol, remember? Nobody jogs here without belonging. So, stay alert, but don't go overboard. Remember what Dad likes to say: There's an important difference between taking precautions and turning paranoid.

She further reassured herself with the thought that she wasn't in this situation alone. As far as she could tell, the Harper Security plan for insinuating operatives into Swann's entourage was working. Kyle had taken up his new job as Swann's driver. Two other agency staffers were working alternating shifts at the recording studio where Nightshade was working on its new record. And, just the other day, Eddie Ramirez, one of the agency's youngest and newest employees, had turned up at the beach house as part of the pool service's weekly cleaning crew. Megan had been out on the deck in her swimsuit with P.J. when they'd arrived. Eddie, whose main assignment seemed to be lugging chemical canisters, had given her a surreptitious wink and muttered something about "nice work if you can get it" as he'd passed.

Nice work, indeed. Deception. Possible danger. And too much close contact with a man who disturbed her very much.

You're a professional, she reminded herself. Colin Swann is your client. Even if he doesn't know it, he is. And professionals don't get involved with their—

"Megan?"

Startled out of her reverie, Megan dropped the screwdriver. She whirled around to confront the man who'd occupied too many of her thoughts during the past two weeks.

Swann bent lithely and retrieved the tool. He was dressed, as he usually was, in black: black running shoes, black jeans, and a black tank top that looked as though it had been sprayed onto his leanly muscled torso. "Boning up on breaking and entering?" he inquired teasingly, handing back the screwdriver.

Megan flushed. "I—of course not! I noticed the lock seemed loose, that's all. I decided to try to fix it." Calm down, she ordered herself. Do you want him to get suspicious? "It's no big deal."

"Mmm." His eyes narrowed slightly. "I—I didn't mean to sneak up on you," he apologized after a moment.

Megan took a deep, steadying breath, trying to maintain her balance. She wondered irritably how a man of Swann's size could make less noise coming into a room than the fog did when it rolled in off the ocean.

"Your mother was right," she declared, hiding her uneasy sense of vulnerability behind a show of asperity. "You *should* wear a bell."

"My mother—?" His dark brows came together during the few seconds it took him to place the reference; then his features cleared. "Oh, the talk on the terrace." He nodded, a hint of a smile teasing one corner of his mouth. "If I recall my fables correctly, there's a certain danger involved in belling the cat."

"Only if you happen to be a mouse," she countered.

It was hardly a typical exchange between nanny and parent. Then again, she was hardly a typical nanny. And Colin Swann certainly wasn't a typical parent. Megan supposed their basic natures—to say nothing of the circumstances of their first meeting—made it impossible for their relationship to develop along orthodox lines.

"You're a lot of things," he drawled, his eyes drifting over her like smoke, "including a few things I haven't figured out yet. But you definitely are *not* a mouse."

She shifted her weight, assuming one of the subtly defensive postures from her martial arts training almost without realizing it. "Yes, well, you're not exactly a common house cat, either."

"No? You can't picture me curled up on your lap and purring?"

So much for defensive postures. She'd left herself wide open for that one.

"Actually, I see you as more predatory than purring," she informed him.

He chuckled, the sound coming out as smooth and mellow as brandy. "And here I was hoping you'd begun to see the real me. A simple, domesticated male."

Megan shook her head. Oh, she'd begun to see him as a *male,* all right. She hadn't been able to overlook his confident, seductive masculinity since waking up beside him after a night she still couldn't fully remember. But as for the two adjectives he'd suggested—

In all honesty, Megan *did* have to admit that Swann was a lot more helpful around the house than she'd expected. Before she'd moved in, she'd mentally braced herself for the possibility that she might be sharing a roof with a sloppy, self-indulgent party animal. She needn't have worried.

Yes, Swann's lifestyle was luxurious. In addition to the pool service, he employed a once-a-week gardener and a twice-a-week cleaning woman. He could afford to live very well, and he did. At the same time, he made his own bed each morning, picked up after himself, and required that his son do the same. Furthermore, he was one of the few men Megan had ever known—including her father, two brothers, and ex-husband—whose notion of doing laundry was more sophisticated than stuffing a pile of unsorted clothes into a washing machine, turning a switch, and hoping for the best. And, on top of everything else, he was a whiz in the kitchen.

"You may be a better cook than I," she conceded,

"but that doesn't make you domesticated."

"I *may* be a better cook?" he mocked lightly, his eyes glinting like polished coins. "This from a woman whose idea of grilling steak is to turn a prime piece of beef into a flaming hunk of shoe leather?"

"Just because you like your meat still mooing is no reason to criticize the way I do steak," she defended herself. "Besides, P.J. thought it was just fine."

"P.J. thinks peanut butter with ketchup is a gourmet treat," Swann reminded her. "And he's hardly an impartial judge, Megan. He'd wolf down Brussels sprouts if *you* served them. As far as he's concerned, you can do no wrong."

Megan smiled. "He wasn't too happy when I told him he couldn't turn his bathroom into a turtle ranch."

"But you made up for it by not throwing a screaming fit when he let Godzilla loose on you the other morning."

Her smile turned into a rippling laugh. "He didn't let him loose on purpose. He was trying to balance Godzilla on his head. Besides, when you consider that I grew up with two brothers who used to drop snakes down my back, having a friendly gerbil scurrying around on me is nothing."

Swann's expression grew thoughtful. "I think that's the first time you've voluntarily mentioned your family since you came," he remarked.

Megan stiffened. For what had to be the hundredth time since she'd moved in, she warned herself about the dangers of letting down her guard around this man. The fewer things she told Swann about herself, the fewer lies she'd have to make up—and remember.

"There isn't much to mention," she answered with feigned casualness. "Two brothers. One mother. One father. I had a happy childhood. Nothing very exciting or unique."

"Mmm." She sensed her withdrawal irritated him . . . and piqued his interest. But he didn't press her. Instinct told her it was only a matter of time before he did. "Well, in any case, you've made a hit with P.J." He lifted his right hand and toyed with one of her red-gold curls. "Like son, like father," he said softly.

His gaze moved slowly, deliberately, from her eyes . . . to her slightly parted lips . . . and back to her eyes. Her breath seemed to thicken, catching in her throat. She felt her heartbeat speed into an irregular rhythm. Color blossomed in her cheeks in response to his scrutiny.

He made no effort to move nearer. He didn't have to. The silken strands of awareness that had linked them from the very start were growing in number and strength, drawing them closer and closer together . . .

"Swann—" She paused, searching for words. She was wearing shorts and a scoop-necked T-shirt. The sun streaming through the glass doors suddenly seemed very warm as it caressed her skin. "Swann, this isn't a good idea."

"I can think of a few arguments in its favor."

"Concentrate on thinking of the ones against it," she counseled, making an effort to follow her own advice. "I work for you, remember? You hired me to take care of P.J. I'm . . . not here to do anything else."

She winced inwardly at the hesitation. Mary Poppins wouldn't have handled the beginning of a pass like this. And neither, she was willing to bet, would have Mrs. Lynton.

One thing this assignment was teaching her was what a lousy con artist she was. The more she got involved— and she *was* getting involved— the guiltier she felt about her deception. There were moments when, caught in her attraction to Swann and her affection for his son, she almost forgot why she was in his house. Then reality would reassert itself, and she would feel more a sham than ever.

A variety of emotions flickered in the changeable depths of Swann's eyes. "I'm not talking about something

I *hired* you to do, Megan," he said. "You're not the type of woman a man tries to buy."

She swallowed. There was an odd edge to the way he said this, as though he'd been exposed to too many women who *were* available for purchase. "I didn't mean—" she began.

"Daddy?" P.J.'s voice piped down from the second floor. This was followed by his *clomp*ing descent down the stairs. While his father moved soundlessly, the six-year-old liked his entrances and exits heralded by as much self-generated noise as possible.

"Saved by the patter of little feet," Swann commented ironically, his mouth twisting. He took a step back.

Megan half laughed, uncertain whether what she was feeling was relief or regret. After fluffing her hair with one hand, she tugged at the bottom of her top.

"Hiya!" P.J. greeted them, jumping off the bottom step. "Hi, Megan!" The "Miss Harper" form of address had been abandoned by mutual consent.

"Hello, P.J.," she said.

P.J. was wearing faded jeans and a partially tucked-in *Star Wars* T-shirt. His dark, shiny hair was mussed. "Did you ask her yet, Dad?" he inquired, hopping toward them.

"I haven't had a chance, buddy."

"Well, are you going to *now?*"

"I guess I'd better." Swann looked at Megan. "I understand you two are going to Griffith Park today," he said, referring to the famed recreation area that sat in the foothills of Santa Monica. Griffith Park sprawled over more than four thousand acres and was the second-largest city-owned park in the world.

Megan nodded, wondering if he had some objection to the idea. "I thought I might take P.J. to the zoo."

"I told you, Daddy!" the little boy chimed in eagerly. "We're going to see the baby animal nursery and *everything!*"

"You don't mind, do you?" Megan asked Swann.

He grinned, suddenly looking very boyish. "Mind? I want to come with you."

Four days later, P.J. was still chattering about the trip to the zoo. Aside from the stomachache he'd acquired by stuffing himself with the wares from various snack stands, he'd had a glorious time. He was already lobbying for a return visit. He was also dropping hints about how much fun it would be to have a walrus.

"But it *was* a fib, right?" he asked Megan, pursuing his point with the zeal of a cross-examining attorney as she helped him climb into his peppermint-stripe-sheeted bed. While the rest of the house was done in subtle tones, P.J.'s room was a riot of primary colors. "When Daddy told that lady at the zoo he was a plumber, that was a *fib*."

"It wasn't the truth," Megan conceded. "But, if he hadn't told her that, she wouldn't have left us alone."

"It was funny when he told her he couldn't be a big rock star because he's tune deaf, huh?"

"*Tone* deaf," she corrected.

"Oh, yeah. Do you ever tell fibs, Megan?" He gazed up at her with wide, innocent eyes.

"Once in a while," she admitted evasively, feeling her heart contract. "Did you brush your teeth?" she asked abruptly.

"Uh-huh." He countered her change of subject with one of his own. "Do you think I'm going to get big?"

"Get big what?" Swann asked, coming into the room. He was carrying an acoustic guitar. Bedtime songs took the place of bedtime stories in the Swann household. "Feet? Ears?"

"No." P.J. giggled. "*Big*. Like that guy by the bear cage."

"What guy by the bear cage?" Megan questioned. P.J. had said something about a big guy once before. For no rational reason, she suddenly thought of the burly jogger on the beach. He'd been out there again that morning, slogging up and down.

"Just this guy. He stared at us a lot. He looked sneaky. I thought maybe he was going to bother you, Daddy. But he didn't. He looked at Megan, too."

Megan bit her lower lip, uneasily aware that she hadn't noticed any big guy staring at them. Was she falling down on the job? Admit it, Megan Louise, she chided herself, the only things you noticed at the zoo were P.J. . . . and Colin Swann. Some undercover bodyguard you are! Proof positive that her attraction to Swann was most unprofessional. A real distraction . . .

"Well, Megan's definitely worth looking at," Swann said smoothly. He glanced across the bed at Megan, giving her a flashing smile that was part adult amusement and part blood-heating approval. Then he sat down on the edge of the mattress. He'd been at the recording studio most of the day. A faint stubble of beard shadowed the planes of his face and he looked tired. "As for getting big—I'll bet you hit at least six feet tall when you grow up."

"I already got *two* feet!" P.J. announced, making a familiar joke. He kicked at the covers to emphasize his point. Then he grew thoughtful. "Mom wasn't big," he observed. Turning his head, he looked at the framed photograph sitting on top of the small table next to his bed.

It was a color portrait, obviously professionally done, of an exquisitely angelic yet extremely sensual blue-eyed blonde. Her name was Iris Ames. A small town unknown who'd won overnight stardom in Hollywood, she'd been Colin Swann's live-in lover and P.J.'s mother. The background information Bernie McGillis had provided on her had been sketchy but unsavory. Iris Ames had deserted her son when he was about four. She died of a drug overdose a year later. In the interim, Swann had secured full legal custody of P.J.

What Swann's true feelings about Iris Ames were, Megan wasn't certain. He didn't discuss them. But clearly he had said nothing against her within his son's hearing. When P.J. mentioned his mother, it was in terms of vague affection. He seemed to have very few real memories of her.

"Your mother was a few inches shorter than Megan," Swann said. "But you'll probably take after me in the height department."

"Hope so."

"Okay. That's settled." Swann shifted his guitar into position and struck a major chord. "Any requests?"

"You have to sit down, too, Megan," P.J. said. After a moment, she seated herself on the bed across from Swann.

"'You Have to Sit Down, Too, Megan,'" Swann repeated teasingly. "I don't think I know that one. Can you hum it?"

P.J. pulled a face. "Dah—dee!" he complained. "Uh—do the friend song, okay?"

"Again?" Swann imitated his son's tone and expression.

"C'mon. *Please?*"

"Only if Megan joins in the chorus." Swann winked at her. "We'll have you singing back-up vocals for Nightshade before too long."

Megan smiled, trying to ignore the sudden rush of tenderness welling up within her. "Don't draw up the contract yet."

Swann took a second to tune one of the guitar strings, his lean fingers deft and sure. Then he strummed the opening bars of the song.

The friend song was a simple, unsophisticated tune with an apparently endless collection of doggerel verses that Swann seemed to make up as he went along.

"Do a walrus," P.J. said, snuggling down in his bed.

His father chuckled, strumming a few more chords, clearly composing in his head. Then he started to sing. The day's recording session had left his voice huskier than usual.

> I have a walrus and his name is Fred.
> Got a big body and a whiskered head.
> He likes to paint his toenails red.
> That's my buddy—my friend Fred.

Swann cued Megan with a nod and she joined him in the chorus.

> He's my friend, and he always will be.
> We're so happy, Fred and me.

On and on the song spun out, until Swann finally sang the verse that meant it was time to say good night. P.J. was half-asleep by then. His father slowed his playing. His voice softened, wrapping around the lyrics like a cashmere blanket.

> Now I want to say to all of you,
> A really friendly "How-do-you-do?"
> And I hope as this song ends,
> You're gonna say we're all good friends.
> We could be friends. I just know we could be.
> We could be happy, you and me.

P.J. yawned into his palm. "I like that song."

"We'll sing more tomorrow," his father promised, leaning forward to kiss him on the forehead. "Good night, buddy."

"'Night, Daddy."

Standing up, Megan took a second to straighten the

sheets. "Sleep tight, P.J.," she said, stroking his dark, silky hair.

"Don't let the bedbugs bite," the little boy responded sleepily. "'Night, Megan."

"You know, you're the best thing to happen to P.J. in a long time," Swann remarked about thirty minutes later. They were sitting companionably downstairs in the living room. The house was quiet. Megan could just hear the rush of the waves of the ocean outside.

Swann had coaxed her into having a drink—non-alcoholic in her case—with him after they'd tiptoed out of P.J.'s room. At first, she'd resisted the idea. The bedtime scene had left her feeling achingly vulnerable, and she'd needed to be alone to shore up her defenses. She'd also wanted to go to her room and check in with her father about the latest developments at the agency. Swann had had a private telephone line installed for her, so she could make calls without fear of being overheard or interrupted.

But she could hardly tell Swann either of those things. So, lacking a plausible excuse for refusing his invitation, she'd given in.

"P.J.'s a terrific little boy," she said sincerely, sipping at her glass of pineapple juice. "It . . . it can't be easy being a single parent. You've done a wonderful job with him."

Swann took a swallow of Scotch. He was in an edgy mood. "Thanks. P.J. is definitely what you'd call a labor of love." His mouth twitched. "Of course, he can be a pain in the neck sometimes, too. But he's something special to me."

"It shows."

He shifted restlessly. They were sitting about a foot and a half apart on a long, multisectioned couch covered in nubby, oatmeal-colored fabric and studded with pillows covered in exotic, handwoven fabrics. Megan had her bare feet curled up under her. Swann's long legs were stretched out in front of him.

"The other day, you said there wasn't very much to mention about your family," he commented reflectively, "that you'd had a happy childhood but nothing—ah—exciting or unique." He ran a hand through his hair. "I hope P.J. will be able to say something like that when he gets older."

Megan drank more of her juice. "You want him to have a childhood . . . different from yours," she suggested slowly.

He looked at her. "Oh, yeah. Not that I was unhappy as a kid. It's just that I don't think the Hollywood hothouse is a healthy environment for a child."

"Before I met him, I half expected P.J. to be a precocious, show-biz brat," she admitted.

"Based, no doubt, on what you knew about me."

"Well—" She veiled her eyes with her lashes, her memory flashing back to their initial meeting. "I probably wasn't what you expected, either."

He laughed as though he were enjoying a private joke on himself. "I'd say *that* was fair."

"I was surprised you even decided to hire me after that first night."

"Mmm." He took another swallow of liquor and then put his glass down. He clearly didn't intend to elaborate on his reasons for hiring her. "This is a strange town, Megan—and I'm in a strange business. It's like a golden Venus's-flytrap. Glittering. Seductive as hell. But it can eat you alive if you're not careful. And it does strange things to people's heads. This is one place where it's not a contradiction—or an insult—to call something . . . someone . . . a genuine phony." He paused. "I want P.J. to grow up being able to tell the real from the fake. It took me a long time to figure out the difference. To be able to see straight. Being in the spotlight tends to mess up your vision, if you know what I mean."

"Not from personal experience, no," she replied.

"And you really don't want to know from personal experience, do you." It wasn't a question. His eyes were a depthless cloud-color as they rested on her. But there was nothing cold or insubstantial about his gaze. There were warily guarded mysteries, yes. But there was also warmth and a heady promise of welcome.

"I'm not harboring any secret desire to be a star," she conceded, running the tip of one finger around the rim of her glass. She had secrets ... desires ... but that wasn't one of them.

His mobile lips curved into a sensual smile. "There's an obvious question I could ask, but I'm going to save you from blushing and not ask it."

"Thank you," she retorted dryly, feeling herself start to flush anyway.

"Do you want children of your own?" he inquired abruptly.

She blinked. "I'd have to get married," she answered, too surprised by the sudden question to censor her response. Then she bit her lip, remembering the out-of-wedlock circumstances of P.J.'s birth. "I didn't mean—" she began to utter hastily.

"I know," he cut in. He gave an odd laugh. "I thought I'd be married, too, if you want the truth."

Megan put down her glass. *The truth.* Was that what she wanted from him? Was that what he wanted from her?

She cleared her throat. Still deliberately avoiding his scrutinizing gaze, she began plucking at a piece of fringe on the russet-and-ivory pillow next to her.

Her job—her *real* job—was to get close to Swann. And that was what was happening. But how could she get close to him and still maintain the professional distance she knew she needed in this situation? Intimacy ... and she couldn't deny it, that was what was growing between them ... wasn't a one-way street. Not for her.

"Megan?" His voice was soft, but his fingers were implacable as they slipped beneath her chin and forced her to look at him. "What are you thinking?" For once, *his* thoughts were clearly readable in his eyes.

She responded to those thoughts—and to the emotions roiling within her.

"I'm thinking this still isn't a good idea." She repeated the assertion she'd made to him four days before, invoking the doubts she had had from the very beginning. What would he do if he knew? she wondered. Perhaps he'd be able to overcome his prejudice about security people. But the deceptions . . . the *lies*—oh, God, she wasn't even a genuine phony!"

"And I can still think of a few arguments in its favor," he returned. "Like . . . this one."

She knew, in the second before he claimed her mouth with his own, that she had been waiting for him to kiss her again. Wanting him to . . . perhaps even needing him to.

His lips were firm yet warmly flexible as they moved over hers. They carried a faint taste of the Scotch he had been drinking. But the flavor of him was distinct and familiar. So was the musky male scent of his skin . . . and the controlled gentleness of the fingers that drifted along her jaw and then tangled possessively in the curls on the back of her head.

This was not like the first kiss he'd given her. And it went beyond the kiss Megan knew they would have shared four days before if P.J. hadn't interrupted. Now, the search of his mouth was rich with intention.

There was hunger in the way he sucked her lower lip into his mouth and then nibbled it until the sensitive flesh tingled. There was demand in the way he teased her with leisurely strokes and probes of his tongue. And there was passion in the way he caressed her body, defining the curves and hollows beneath her clothes.

She felt herself begin to go as pliant as wax over a

flame. He melted her with one skilled touch and then molded her with another. Desire dictated, and mutual pleasure, mutually given, was irresistible.

Swann courted her with his knowing singer's mouth and coaxed her with his experienced musician's fingers. He awoke her, aroused her...

Blood thrummed in her ears in stereo. Yet, through the roar of it, she could hear the moist sounds of their kisses and the irregular pattern of her breathing. Swann began tracking the line of her throat with his lips. His breath searing, he said something deep in his throat against her quivering skin. She couldn't make out the words, but the feel of them being spoken made her tremble.

She barely registered the metallic snap as he undid the fastener at the top of her shorts... or the raspy whisper as he pulled down the zipper. She was only dimly aware of the sudden easing of the garment's snug fit. Realization of what he had done—of how far they had gone—hit her when she felt his fingers straying across her stomach. Her muscles contracted as he stroked the indentation of her navel and then moved lower still, toying with the lace-trimmed top of her underpants.

Perhaps her reaction was a legacy from high school necking sessions—sessions in which she had imposed very definite and decidedly conservative territorial boundaries. Megan didn't know. She didn't really care. All that mattered was that this situation was on the verge of getting totally out of control and that it was up to her to call a halt, *now*... while she still could.

"Swann—" Her voice came out like sandpaper.

His fingers had stilled the moment she'd started to resist, but they remained only inches away from the most intimate part of her body. He said nothing, just stared at her, waiting. The pupils of his eyes were dilated, like medallions of onyx rimmed in silver. There was an uncharacteristic stiffness to his posture as though he were holding himself in check.

"I—we can't," she told him, squirming away from his touch as best she could. Lord, she could only imagine what she looked like!

"Can't?" The mocking skepticism in his voice dissected her protest like a stiletto.

"I work for you!" she said, her tone soft but intense.

Something stirred in his eyes. "If that's the problem," he replied caressingly, "then you're fired."

"Wh—what?" She felt as though she'd been kicked in the stomach.

"But only until tomorrow morning," he went on huskily, a smile teasing his lips. "Then I'll rehire you."

She went absolutely cold. Her expression must have betrayed her shock, too, because she saw his face alter in response to whatever he was reading in hers.

Swann swore. "Megan, I didn't mean that the way it came out," he said urgently.

She knew, deep down, that he was telling the truth. She wasn't certain if that made things better or worse. For the moment, however, she grabbed the most hurtful interpretation of his bantering words, willing herself to feel angry and insulted. She could say *no* now . . . and make it stick.

"You didn't mean to let me know all you want from me is a one-night stand?" she demanded.

"All I want from you—" he echoed, his voice taut. "Megan, no—"

"No, is right!" she said in a hiss. She scooted away from him and scrambled off the couch. Shaking, she tried to restore some order to her clothes. "No *now* . . . and no *tomorrow morning.*"

She half expected him to try to stop her, to try to change her mind. But he remained seated, watching her, his eyes vivid with emotion in a face that suddenly seemed set in stone.

She swallowed. "I'm going upstairs now," she informed him, her words as stiff as her body, and she turned on her heel.

"Megan."

It was like a touch. It bridged the distance between them, half command, half plea . . . wholly irresistible.

She turned back.

"I want a hell of a lot more from you than a one-night stand," he said. For a moment she thought her heart had stopped.

You're a professional, Megan Louise. Act like one!

"I take care of your son, Mr. Swann," she declared, the words coming out as clear and sharp as etched glass. Her heart started beating again. "Good night."

Many hours later, as she tossed sleeplessly in her bed, she asked herself what she wanted from him . . . and who was going to take care of her.

CHAPTER FOUR

YAWNING WEARILY, MEGAN finished scraping and rinsing the breakfast plates and began to load them into the dishwasher with mechanical precision. She felt like the "before" part of a commercial for a cure for iron-poor blood. Tense and tired...

"Well, I'm glad I'm not the only one who had trouble sleeping last night."

Megan jumped. P.J.'s Darth Vader milk mug slipped from her wet hands and fell to the floor. Fortunately, it was plastic. It bounced and didn't break. Too bad she wasn't quite so resilient.

"Don't you believe in knocking?" she demanded, bending quickly to retrieve the cup. She straightened up.

Swann was standing six feet away. He was wearing track shoes, shorts, and a faded Nightshade T-shirt. He'd evidently been running on the beach. From the looks of him, it had been a long, hard run.

"This is my house," he pointed out in a tone that was about as reasonable as a block of granite.

Megan stuffed P.J.'s mug into the dishwasher with a careless thrust, nearly impaling herself on a fork in the process. "At least clear your throat when you come into a room," she suggested ungraciously, rubbing her hand. "Heart failure is not my idea of getting the day off to a great start." Lord, less than a minute ago, she'd been dragged out and depressed. Now there was enough adrenaline pumping through her veins to send her into overdrive.

"I'm sorry," he said, stripping off the shirt. He wiped his chest with it. The lean, sweat-sheened muscles of his torso rippled smoothly with the movement. The dark, crisp hair on his bronzed chest clung to his skin in a matted pattern of whorls. "Where's P.J.?"

Megan glanced away from him for a moment, telling herself it was her nerves—and nothing else—that were making her so acutely aware of each detail of his appearance. "He's upstairs cleaning Godzilla's cage." Weekly cleanings were on the schedule she'd organized for the little boy. She slammed the dishwasher door shut with more force than was needed.

"Good. Then we've got a few minutes to talk."

"About what?"

"Last night."

Megan wiped the palms of her hands on her white duck shorts. "I don't want to talk about last night."

"I do."

"Last night was last night. It's over. Just forget it."

"Can you?"

"Can I what?"

"Can you just forget it?" he asked. His eyes were like steel rivets, nailing her where she stood.

"Yes."

His mouth curved. It wasn't so much a smile as a

baring of teeth. "You're not a very good liar," he told her softly.

You'd be surprised, she thought with a spurt of anger. "I'm not lying," she denied.

"I don't think you can just forget last night anymore than I can." He went on as though she hadn't spoken.

"Swann, I work—"

"And don't throw your job in my face."

She clenched her hands into fists. She'd like to throw more than her job in his face! "Have you ever heard of sexual harassment?" she inquired, searching for some defense.

Something—a very strange mixture of anger and admiration—shone in the depths of his eyes. "Megan, this is definitely sexual, but it is *not* harassment."

"No? Then what is it?"

There was a short silence. For no reason she could explain, Megan found herself feeling like one of those Saturday morning cartoon characters who takes a second or two to realize he's run off the edge of a cliff and is standing in midair, about to plunge to the ground.

"I don't think I'm ready to answer that," Swann told her slowly. "And I don't think you'd want me to, even if I were."

Megan bit her lip. "Has it ever occurred to you that I might not . . . want what you want?" she asked.

"No," he responded simply.

For a moment, Megan just gaped. "Of all the—the *conceited*—!" she sputtered furiously. God, even if it *hadn't* occurred to him, she hadn't thought he'd have the gall to admit it to her.

"That was experience, not arrogance, speaking," he cut in smoothly. "I'm thirty-five years old, Megan. I lost my virginity a long time ago. And my innocence about life a couple of years before that. I know when a woman is attracted to me."

"And you *know* I'm attracted to you." She tried to sound scathing. She barely made it to skeptical.

"Yes," he confirmed flatly. "And you know damned well *I'm* attracted to *you*."

During the course of this exchange, Swann had moved to within touching distance of her. Now he put his hands on her shoulders. His palms curved to match the shape of her flesh; his thumbs came to rest lightly on her collarbone.

She looked at him, chin tilted and cheeks flushed. "Even if I—if we . . . I've told you before—"

"That this is not a good idea," he completed. "Why, Megan? It feels good. It feels *right*." His eyes pored over her face as though he were trying to puzzle out a very difficult passage in a unique manuscript. "Look, I admit I've earned myself a pretty wild reputation over the years. But I'm not—I'm not going to hurt you."

Oh yes, you are, Megan thought with a pang, because I've already betrayed your basic-level trust—and whatever else you may feel for *me*. And when you find that out, no matter how much I try to explain that it was for your own good, you're going to wasnt to hurt back. It's only human.

She closed her eyes for a moment. "I can't handle this, Swann," she said with absolute—if incomplete—truthfulness. She opened her eyes a second later when she felt the stroke of his fingers on her cheek.

"I think you can handle just about anything, Megan," he replied.

It wasn't a line. She'd been handed enough of those in her life to know one when she heard one. It wasn't even an attempt to flatter her into changing her mind, although his touch and tone were subtly seductive. No, this was a simple statement of fact as he saw it . . . as he saw *her*.

"No. Not *this*," she repeated with conviction. "Not . . . now."

He let go of her. It wasn't rejection; it was release.

"You need time," he said. His manner was very steady, very controlled.

She nodded. *Yes,* she needed time! Time to find out who was sending him threatening letters. Time to figure out how to tell him who she really was and what she really did. Time to sort out her feelings...

He slung his shirt over his shoulder and forked his hand back through his hair. "Okay," he said decisively.

"Okay," he repeated. "Look, Megan, I'm not going to rush you into something you're not sure about—although we both know I probably *could* rush you..."

He paused, obviously expecting her to react. Megan remained silent. How could she deny his assertion when the memory of his kisses still throbbed in her mind?

"So, I can wait," he went on. "I've learned the hard way that you can't avoid the inevitable. And you can't hurry what's never going to happen."

Although his voice was perfectly smooth, Megan heard the razor-sharp edge of bitterness buried in the philosophic words. She wondered how much Iris Ames had had to do with Colin Swann's learning the hard way.

"It may be a long time," she said after a few seconds. She wasn't being coy or challenging; she was simply being honest. As honest as she could be right now.

Swann smiled. "I'm a professional musician, remember? I know how to wait for my cue." He brushed the slightly callused tips of his fingers lightly against her lips. "And I know how to pick it up when it comes." He paused, cocking his head. "And, speaking of cues—"

The *thump-clump* of P.J.'s footsteps punctuated this remark. A moment later, the little boy bounded into the kitchen as bright and bouncy as a beach ball.

"Okay, I cleaned Godzilla's cage just like you told me to, Megan," he announced without preamble. "P.U. *Gross!*"

"Did you wash your hands?" Megan inquired. Like

many six-year-old boys, P.J. had a distinct aversion to soap and water.

"Um." P.J. wrinkled his nose. "Sort of."

"Sort of?" his father echoed with a note of disapproval.

The little boy put out his hands for a few seconds, palms up. "See, they're clean," he asserted. "I wiped them on a towel."

Swann and Megan exchanged glances. Megan could feel the tension between them ease. No matter how many other things divided them, they would always be drawn together by the affection they shared for P.J.

"I'll remind the cleaning service to be sure to change the linens again," she said resignedly. P.J. and his best friend, seven-year-old Joey Guarino, had created their own version of personalized towels earlier in the week with fingerpaints.

"I didn't get the towel *that* dirty," P.J. protested quickly. "Anyway, I folded it so nothing shows." He tugged at the bottom of his striped jersey for a moment, his eyes darting from Megan to his father and back again. "Um . . . only maybe you better tell the cleaning lady she doesn't have to do my room this time."

"And why is that, Peej?" Swann inquired in a calm voice.

"Well . . ." P.J. rocked back on his heels. "Um, Godzilla, well, got out while I was fixing his cage."

"He's loose in your room again," Megan translated.

"I'll catch him," P.J. promised immediately. "He probably just want to play around for a while. His cage is pretty dinky, you know. I'll bet he got tired of it. I put some gerbil food on the floor, so he won't get hungry."

"P.J.—" Megan started to remonstrate.

"He'll be okay," the little boy assured her blithely. "It's like at the zoo. Remember, Daddy? You said it wasn't mean to put the animals there because it was like their natural hobby—habi—where they live."

"I don't think your room qualifies as a gerbil's natural habitat," his father said.

"Yeah, but—"

"P.J., let's go upstairs and find Godzilla," Megan interrupted. *"Now."*

The little boy sighed. "Okay. Hey—maybe we can get Godzilla a *bell!* That way, next time he gets . . . Megan? Daddy? What's so funny?"

"Dad? It's Megan."

"How's it going, Meg?" Simon Harper's familiar voice came through the phone line in a gravelly rumble. It was a voice that could scold or soothe with equal facility.

"Quiet," she admitted, stretching out on the jade and peach quilted coverlet on her queen-size bed as she twisted the telephone cord around her finger. "We did have some excitement. P.J.'s gerbil nearly got sucked up by a vacuum cleaner."

"Oh?"

"The gerbil survived. The cleaning lady quit."

Simon Harper's chuckle was low and appreciative. "Sounds like when Kyle tried to flush your cat down the toilet."

"Something like that." Megan stifled a yawn. P.J. had been tucked into bed an hour before. Swann, as far as she knew, was still at the recording studio. "Speaking of Kyle, how's he holding up as Swann's chauffeur? He certainly seems to be throwing himself into the role. He actually tipped his cap to me the other day." In an effort to avoid arousing Swann's suspicion, she and her brother had agreed to limit their contact.

"You know Kyle. He really digs in when he works undercover." Megan heard the pride in her father's voice. She knew he had dug in when he'd been on the L.A. police force. Simon Harper had been on an undercover assignment when a drug dealer's bullet had crippled him and ended his police career. "To tell the truth, I think he's finding this job a little dull. Colin Swann isn't quite the high-living rock star he expected."

"He's disappointed because there haven't been any orgies in the back seat of the limo, right?" Megan surmised, thinking that Swann hadn't turned out to be quite what she'd expected, either.

"That's about the size of it."

"Kyle's probably been hoping he could latch on to a few leftover groupies," she observed wryly.

"Probably," her father agreed.

There was a short pause. Megan rubbed the top of her head, sighing to herself.

"Is there anything new on the letter that came yesterday?" she asked finally, her expression growing serious. This one had been much more ominous than the one before. It had included several obscenely graphic threats plus a magazine picture of Swann that had been shredded to bits. And, even more worrisome, it bore the postmark of a city even closer than the last: Phoenix.

Chicago, Illinois. Phoenix, Arizona. *I'm coming for you*.

"No, nothing new," her father replied, his tone turning businesslike. "But we're going to keep digging. In the meantime, you just sit tight on the inside."

"I . . . this waiting—the not knowing whether there really is somebody out there—"

"There really is somebody out there," Simon Harper told her grimly. "Whether he intends to do something is another matter."

"You think he does, don't you?"

"Meg, there's no certainty in a case like this. But I've seen enough of this sort of thing—these letters are very directed, very personal. And I do get the feeling that whoever's writing them is trying to goad himself as well as get at Swann. In the meantime, you just stay cool, just keep doing what you've been doing."

But I don't *know* what I've been doing! she wanted to scream. To confess.

"Yes, sir," she said instead, "but once this job is over, I'd just as soon go back to my regular type of assignment. I don't think I'm cut out for undercover work."

"You're doing fine," he reassured her. Then, in an obvious attempt to ease her mood, he remarked, "I'll bet you're doing plenty of leg work, running after Swann's son."

"A fair amount," Megan conceded, willing herself to relax a little.

"Your mother always said taking care of you kids kept her in shape. She's put on a few pounds, you know, since you all grew up. Now, if she had a few more grand—"

"Let's not get started on that again, please." It was a familiar theme. Her brother Steve had three children and that was all he and his wife, Lynda, wanted. Her brother Kyle was too busy playing the field to think about fatherhood. And she . . . well, she truly did want children. But, as she'd told Swann, she stuck to the old-fashioned conviction that she should be a wife before she went about becoming a mother.

Looking back, she now realized that the dream of having children of her own had been one reason she'd rushed into marriage with Doug. Oh, she'd genuinely loved him, although she was honest enough with herself to admit that she hadn't really known him. And Doug had loved her, too, in his way. Unfortunately, his way had had very little to do with remaining faithful or starting a family.

Considering how their marriage had ended, it probably was just as well that there hadn't been any children.

"Well—" Once he'd broached a subject, Simon Harper didn't give it up easily. "Meg, isn't it about time you started—"

"Is there anything else?" Megan asked pointedly. She

adored her father, but she was feeling too unsettled to tolerate this kind of parental prodding.

"Okay, okay. I get the message. Your mother checked your apartment for you. She did a little dusting."

Megan had to laugh. She knew her mother's definition of *a little dusting*. "How much of my furniture did she rearrange?"

"Oh, a few things here and there."

"Well, tell her thanks. She probably scrubbed the kitchen floor, too."

"I seem to remember her mentioning that, yes."

"I'll bet. Well, I'll call you tomorrow. 'Night, Dad."

"'Night, honey."

A week later, Megan lay out by the pool, soaking up the sun along with Patti Guarino. P.J. and Joey Guarino were in the water, shouting and splashing.

Megan had gotten to know the members of Swann's band, plus their various families and hangers-on, fairly well since starting work as P.J.'s nanny. P.J.'s friendship with Joey had made it inevitable that she would end up spending a great deal of time with Patti. Fortunately, she'd taken to Coney's hardheaded but warm-hearted wife immediately. For her part, Patti seemed to treat Megan like a long-lost sister.

At the moment, Patti was discussing the problems of having a fifteen-year-old daughter who was about to go out on her first date. Megan had just finished applying sunscreen.

"I think I'm handling the situation very well," Patti remarked, patting her chronically uncoiffed salt-and-pepper hair. She had it scraped back into a ponytail at the moment. Short, plump, and blithely indifferent to fashion trends where her own appearance was concerned, Patti Guarino was about as far from the stereotype of a celebrity wife as a woman could get. "Do you learn how to handle these older kid problems in nanny school?"

She looked at Megan reflectively. "Coney," she added, "is going to pieces."

"I always thought it would take an earthquake to shake him." Megan smiled. Coney was the oldest and most settled member of Nightshade. He was a slight man with dreamy-eyed face. His most distinguishing feature was a drooping Zapata mustache.

"He's carrying on like Lisa's date is a junior version of Rick Nichols."

Megan laughed. She'd quickly learned that Rick Nichols, the band's bass guitarist, went through women like Kleenex. Several years before, a gossip columnist had started referring to each successive girlfriend as "Nichols's latest flavor of the Month." The nickname had stuck.

"I suppose it's hard for a father to see his little girl grow up," she commented, thinking of how her father had reacted when she'd started going out with boys. There had been times when Simon Harper's version of getting acquainted with her dates had sounded perilously close to a third-degree grilling of a felony suspect. She lay back on the chaise longue.

"Maybe. Personally, I think Coney's remembering all the hell-raising he used to do with *other* fathers' little girls," Patti said, her dark eyes sparkling as she gave one of her rich, michievous laughs.

"Coney?" Megan lifted her head.

"Oh, I know he looks and acts like a devoted basset hound now, but he did more than his share of baying at the moon—so to speak—before we got married." Patti examined her short, unpolished nails. "And how are things on the Malibu front?" It was, for her, a fairly subtle opening bid for information.

Megan winced as P.J. performed a belly flop off the side of the pool. "Nobody's been baying at the moon—so to speak," she replied mildly. Actually, things had been going quite well at the beach house . . . considering.

Certainly, her relationship with Swann was considerably more relaxed than it had been before their confrontation in the kitchen. Of course, the powerful tug of physical and emotional attraction was still there. But at least Swann was sticking to his promise to give her the time she needed.

"Uh-huh." Patti pursed her lips, obviously deciding to rebait her conversational hook before going on with her fishing expedition. "You do realize that people have been—ah—*wondering* about you and Swann," she said eventually.

"Any people in particular?"

"Mmm . . . the guys in the band."

"Patti—" Megan levered herself up on her elbows and looked at the other woman. Patti had nibbled around the edges of this issue several times before. Megan suspected she was about to sink her teeth into it now.

"Oh, all right." Patti grimaced good-naturedly as she adjusted the strap of her swimsuit. *"I've* been wondering about you and Swann. Not that I'm the only one, you understand, but—"

"But there's nothing to wonder about. I work for Swann. I take care of P.J. I'm just like Mrs. Lynton."

Patti gave a hoot of laughter. "Believe me, you are *nothing* like Edwina Lynton."

"You mean you didn't wonder about her and Swann?" Megan inquired with a trace of sarcasm.

"Are you kidding? I wouldn't have dared! She scared me to death. She was so—so—*proper.*"

"You know, the more I hear about her, the less I understand why Swann hired her," Megan commented truthfully.

"I think his mother helped pick her. She's big on British nannies. Mrs. Lynton arrived—oh—about six months after Iris walked out. Everything was—well, I suppose Swann wanted someone who'd give P.J. plenty of stability. God knows, Mrs. Lynton was *stable*. The woman was as solid as the Rock of Gibraltar—and I'm not just talking about the way she was built."

"Did . . . you know P.J.'s mother well?" Megan asked slowly, almost reluctantly. She could have tried to tell herself that her curiosity was professional—that the more she knew about the people who touched Swann's life, the better she'd be able to protect him. But that would have been a lie, and she knew it. Her reasons for wanting to know about Iris Ames were purely personal.

Patti sighed. "I knew her. I didn't like her. She was self-centered, careless . . . a real user."

"Did she use Swann?"

"Oh, yes—although he'd never admit to it. Look, she was gorgeous. But once you got past that, which took a little time, considering how blindingly beautiful she was, she didn't have a lot to offer someone like Swann. She was smart enough to realize that, so she got pregnant with P.J. Swann may look like a pirate, but he's got a big streak of white knight in him—"

"He's got a sense of honor," Megan said softly, thinking back to the conversation she'd had with Bernie McGillis. The cowboy code . . . the Round Table . . . the samurai system.

"Exactly." Patti nodded emphatically. "He's . . . oh, old-fashioned, I guess is as good a way as any to put it. Let's face it, in this day and age, a lot of guys would have told Iris to take a hike." She frowned. "A lot of guys probably would have asked if the baby was even *theirs*—"

"You mean—?" Megan was honestly shocked. Her eyes flew toward P.J. He and Joey were now standing in the shallow end of the pool, throwing a ball back and forth.

"She slept around," Patti said bluntly. "I don't know. P.J. is Swann's son legally . . . and emotionally. And that's really all that matters." Sighing, she shook her head. "Oh, I suppose you can find excuses for the way Iris

was. She lost her parents when she was a kid. The welfare
people split her and her brother into different foster families. She grew up wanting things . . . attention. And then
she came to Hollywood and *boom;* she became the blonde
of the year. It couldn't have been easy. But, still . . ."
She sighed again. "I'm sorry she's dead. But I'm not
sorry she's out of Swann's life—or P.J.'s."

Megan sat up, suddenly wishing she hadn't encour-
aged Patti to talk so frankly. She wanted to learn about
Swann—all about Swann. But not like this. Not behind
his back.

"Megan?" Patti questioned, sitting up, too.

"Nothing . . . it's nothing."

"Do you . . . ever wonder about yourself and Swann?"
the other woman asked after a few seconds.

Megan looked at her. The conversation, inevitably,
had come full circle. "He's very attractive," she replied.

"He's more than that. And so are you." Patti's dark
eyes were very serious, very steady.

"Patti—" For a moment, the temptation to confide
the truth was so strong, she could practically feel the
words forming in her throat. She choked them back.
"There are . . . complications."

"Complications?"

"Yes. I can't—the time just isn't right."

Patti's mouth curved into a knowing female smile.
There was an odd hint of conspiracy in her expression.
It reminded Megan of the smile Alexandra Collins had
given her that day on the terrace.

"Don't worry," Coney's wife said. "It will be."

Megan was still thinking about what Patti had said
several hours later when she opened the front door of
the beach house to Alexandra Collins.

"Lady Swann!" she exclaimed. "I—"

"I hope I'm not interrupting anything," the actress
said. She looked characteristically elegant in a lovely

sapphire silk ensemble. A uniformed chauffeur stood a step or two behind her, holding a cardboard box. "Colin said you've worked out a daily schedule for P.J.—"

"No, you're not interrupting anything," Megan assured her quickly. "P.J.'s going to a birthday party later this week, and we were upstairs wrapping his present.

"Oh, good." Swann's mother signaled the chauffeur. "Please put the box inside the door, Alan," she said, stepping gracefully into the house as Megan moved aside to allow her to enter. The driver followed his employer's instructions silently, then touched the brim of his hat, and left.

Megan glanced curiously at the cardboard box. The top of it was punctured with holes and there were sounds of scrabbling and whimpering coming from inside it. She looked at the actress.

The older woman smiled. "Yes, it's a puppy," she said. "And I've already told Colin. I was out shopping earlier today and I saw him—the puppy—and I simply couldn't resist. I do hope P.J. likes him."

Megan laughed. "I'm sure P.J. will love him." Turning, she called the little boy's name. Then she faced Alexandra again. "I'm sorry we haven't been over to visit recently, but you'd mentioned how busy you were going to be with preproduction on your new movie—"

"You're sweet to call it *my* movie. The truth is, my name isn't even above the title. It's a very glamorous kind of cameo, really. But, there *has* been a lot to do, I must admit."

"Grandma Sandra!" P.J. skipped into the foyer. He'd decorated the front of his slightly grubby T-shirt with pieces of Scotch tape.

"Hello, darling." His grandmother accepted his enthusiastic, skirt-mussing hug without objection.

"Me and Megan were wrapping a birthday present," he told her. "Megan had this real neat idea about making our own wrapping paper. It turned out *great*. Megan knows how to do lots of good stuff." He gave Megan a grin and then looked back at his grandmother. "Did you come to see me?" he inquired with the innocent self-centeredness of childhood.

"Well, actually, I had a delivery to make." P.J.'s grandmother gestured at the box. "It is something for you."

"Me?" Megan saw his eyes widen slightly. "What—what is it?"

"Why don't you open it and find out?"

The little boy needed no further encouragement. He stopped, gasping with delight once he yanked the top open and saw what was inside. A few seconds later, he had his arms filled with a squirming puppy. "Oh, wow!" he repeated over and over, beaming. "Oh, wow! He's for *me?* A real *dog?*"

"He's a cocker spaniel and he's about seven weeks old," Alexandra informed him.

P.J. nuzzled a cheek against the puppy's wavy, golden-brown coat. "A cocker spaniel! Oh, boy—Megan, isn't he *neat?* You want to pet him?"

Megan accepted the invitation. "He certainly is neat, P.J.," she said sincerely, stroking the puppy's silken head. "But don't squeeze too hard."

"I won't," he promised, still cradling the animal. He giggled happily as the puppy licked him. "His tongue tickles!"

"Don't you have something to say to your grandmother?" Megan prompted after a few seconds.

"Huh—oh!" He gazed up at his grandmother. "Hey, *thanks*, Grandma Sandra. My very own puppy! Thanks! And can I name him and everything?"

"You can name him and everything," Alexandra assured him with a fond smile.

"Then I'm going to call him Buddy," P.J. decided instantly. "Like Daddy calls me sometimes. Oh, wow. *Buddy.*" He hugged the puppy again, but not too hard. "Your name is Buddy, okay?" he crooned. Amazingly, the animal gave a vaguely affirmative *yip*. The little boy look appealingly at Megan. "Can I take Buddy upstairs to meet Godzilla?" he implored hopefully.

"Well—"

"Ah—Buddy's not housebroken," Alexandra said.

"I won't let him make a mess," P.J. said quickly. "And if he does, I'll clean it all up. Because he's *my* puppy." He looked at his grandmother. "See, Megan says if you have a pet, you have to take care of it," he explained seriously. "Even if it means doing yucky stuff." He glanced at Megan. "Can I—?"

"You can take Buddy up to meet Godzilla," Megan told him. "But don't take Godzilla out of his cage when you're introducing them."

"Yippee! C'mon, Buddy. Let's go see Godzilla."

"Well, that seems to have worked out," Alexandra declared with a satisfied laugh after the little boy disappeared with his new pet. "I hope this won't present any problems for you. The pup—excuse me, *Buddy's* had all his shots and he's been checked by a vet."

"I'm sure there'll be no problem," Megan said, still warmed by her six-year-old charge's happiness. "P.J.'s been very good about looking after Godzilla. I know he'll do fine with Buddy, too."

The actress tilted her head slightly, assessing Megan. "*Megan says* and *Megan knows*," she murmured. "Those seem to be two of P.J.'s favorite phrases these days."

"I hear a lot of *Daddy says* and *Daddy knows*."

"Still—you've obviously made yourself an important part of my grandson's life."

Megan glanced away for a moment, not wanting to betray the contradictory emotions the other woman's words stirred in her. She was touched by the approval she heard in Alexandra's voice, but, at the same time, she was torn by the knowledge that she'd become a part of P.J. Swann's life only through a deception. A necessary deception, true, but a deception nonetheless. "Thank you," she said quietly, meeting Alexandra's blue eyes again. She summoned up a smile. "Would you like to come in and sit down? I could fix you something to drink—"

"Oh, no. No, thank you. I really have to be running along. But—I take it Colin isn't here?"

Megan shook her head. "He's at the recording studio."

"Ah." Alexandra nodded and then confessed, "You know, when P.J. was staying with me, I saw my son every day. And, before that, I kept track of him—more or less—through the gossip columns. But lately—"

"He's been working very hard," Megan stated, not quite certain where the conversation was heading.

"And staying at home most of the time when he isn't."

"Well—"

"Not without good reason, of course."

Megan shifted. "Lady Swann—" she began to say.

"Alexandra, please."

"I don't—"

"I saw a picture of you, Colin, and P.J. at the zoo," the actress went on complacently, patting her silver hair. "It was in one of those wretched tabloids."

Megan felt her cheeks grow hot. Some photographer—probably an enterprising amateur—had snapped a picture of them at one point during their outing at Griffith Park. Swann had been far more irritated by its publication than he had been by the pestering attentions of the woman he'd lied to about being a plumber. "Your son wasn't very happy about it," she conceded cautiously, still not sure what the point of all this was.

"He values his privacy. Still, it was a very attractive photograph . . . not quite the image of him the public is used to seeing." Alexandra paused for a moment. "Several people have remarked on it, in fact."

"Excuse me?"

Swann's mother gave her a limpid look. "It's only to be expected. You, living here—" she said. "There *has* been speculation."

Megan blinked. *What* was going on? Alexandra Collins didn't seem at all upset. If anything, she seemed smug. Even knowing—

"You haven't been talking to Patti Guarino, have you?" Megan asked suddenly.

The older woman looked blank. "Patti—oh, Coney's wife. No. Not recently. Why?"

Megan hesitated for a second and then decided to plunge ahead. "Because earlier today, *she* said there's been speculation about me and your son," she declared wryly.

"Ah." Alexandra gave her smooth coiffure another unnecessary pat. "I must say that Patti's always struck me as a very perceptive woman," she remarked.

"Lady Swann—"

"Alexandra, *please*."

"All right. *Alexandra*. I don't see—"

"You will," came the maddeningly enigmatic assurance. "But, now, I *do* have to be dashing off." She glanced upward. "I take it the introduction of Godzilla and Buddy must be going well."

"I'm sure it's the start of a beautiful friendship," Megan said, "but—"

"Don't worry, my dear. Everything will be fine." Alexandra's expression changed suddenly, hardening slightly. A hint of steeliness entered her blue eyes and her mouth thinned. Her usual air of serenity took on a tinge of grimness. *"Everything."*

"Alexandra—?" Megan felt a prickle of apprehension. "Is something wrong?"

The other woman's fine-featured face cleared immediately. "No. No, not at all," she said, her flawlessly painted lips forming a brief but warm smile. "I—I just have a great deal on my mind. You understand."

No, Megan didn't. "Are you sure?" she asked.

"Quite certain, yes," was the firm but gracious response. "Now, I must go." Her expression altered once again. "Megan—"

"Yes?"

"If—if there's ever anything I can do, Megan, please call me."

Megan had the distinct feeling this was more than an empty courtesy. For the second time she wondered just how much Lady Swann might know. "I will," she said.

"Good-bye for now, my dear."

Megan frowned. "Good-bye." she said.

A day later, Swann received another letter. As with the preceding letters, the words of hate were scrawled in black Magic Marker on a cheap sheet of paper. Again it accused Swann of never having loved "her."

The envelope it came in held the savagely ripped up pieces of a publicity photo from the Colin Swann Official Fan Club.

The envelope was postmarked Los Angeles.

CHAPTER FIVE

P.J.'S NORMALLY CHEERFUL face was crumpled into a look of childish concern.

"Is something wrong, Megan?" he asked anxiously, surveying her with wide eyes. It was shortly after noon, and the two of them were sitting in a fast-food restaurant having lunch after a visit to his dentist.

Experiencing a flash of guilt, Megan summoned what she hoped was a reassuring smile. Never underestimate the perceptivity of a six-year-old, she reminded herself.

"Everything's just fine, P.J.," she said, pleating her straw wrapper between her fingers. She hated the fake brightness of her tone.

Everything *wasn't* fine. The thought of the letter postmarked L.A. was making her distinctly edgy. She hadn't slept well, and her usual composure was as frayed as the collar on a cheap cotton shirt.

"Really and truly?" the little boy pressed. He paused in the act of peeling the top half of the bun off his hamburger. "You been acting weird lately."

Megan took a deep breath, trying to relax. She wasn't doing herself—or P.J.—any good getting keyed up like this. She exhaled slowly. "I'm a little preoccupied, that's all," she explained.

P.J. finished dismantling his sandwich. After carefully removing the pickle slices, he licked his ketchup-covered fingers and then reassembled the hamburger.

"What's preoccupied?" he wanted to know.

"It means I have things on my mind."

"Oh." He took a slurping drink of his chocolate milkshake while he digested this definition. "Daddy's been acting weird, too," he declared after a few moments. "Does he have things on *his* mind?"

"Well—" Megan took a sip of her soda. She'd barely seen Swann during the past four days. He'd been at the recording studio most of the time. She'd missed him. "You know how busy he's been working on the new Nightshade album."

"Yeah, I guess." P.J. picked up his hamburger and took a large bite from it. He chewed slowly, his expression thoughtful.

Megan glanced around the restaurant, wishing she could shake the uneasy feeling that had been gnawing at the edges of her consciousness all morning. Everything in the immediate vicinity seemed normal. Several tables away, a pair of teenage girls were giggling and gossiping over large diet sodas. At the table next to them, a harried young mother was trying to negotiate the division of a box of french fries among her three raucous children. Across the way, a glum man in a business suit was chewing a fish sandwich as he scanned the *Wall Street Journal*.

A typical lunch crowd for this sort of place. Nothing unusual. Nothing suspicious—

Out of the corner of her eye, she caught sight of a burly man sliding into a booth on the opposite side of the restaurant. Her stomach twisted into a knot as she

realized who it was. The jogger from the beach! There
was no mistaking his bulk or the tanklike quality of his
movements. And there was no mistaking his looking
directly at their table as he seated himself.

"Megan?" P.J. asked through a mouthful of french
fries.

She moistened her lips with the tip of her tongue,
telling herself not to get carried away. There were probably a dozen harmless explanations for the man's presence . . . and for why he kept glancing toward them.

"Megan, you look funny."

"P.J.—" Her mind was racing through possibilities,
but she kept her voice very casual. Oh, Lord, she thought.
What if—? "Ah . . . P.J., do you—do you remember the
man at the zoo you told me about? The big man by the
bear cage?"

He blinked, obviously puzzled. "Yeah. Sort of."

"Do you think you'd recognize him if you saw him
again?" She had no rational reason to connect this man
with the one at the zoo, of course. Just a hunch. But
Megan had learned the value of hunches in her profession; they'd saved her time and trouble on more than one
occasion.

"Rec'nize?"

"Like on the adventure show you and Joey were
watching on TV the other day? When the hero spotted
the bank robber—"

"Oh, yeah! He *fingered* him. That was really neat,
huh? And then he—"

"Right, P.J.," she interrupted him gently. "Do you think
you'd recognize the man from the zoo?"

The little boy shrugged. "I don't know. Maybe. I
remember he was really big. And he had little squinty
eyes. Like that director Grandma Sandra doesn't like
because he wanted her to play an old lady. And, oh yeah,
he looked really sneaky, too."

"Good. That's very good." The man on the other side

of the restaurant *did* have little squinty eyes ... and a furtive air.

"But, how come—"

"P.J., there's a big man sitting across from us in a booth next to the wall. He's near the poster of Ronald McDonald. He has brownish hair and a tan sports jacket. I want you to turn your head very slowly and tell me if you think he's the man from the bear cage."

The youngster stared at her. "Is he a *bad guy?*" he asked in a hushed voice. He sounded more excited than apprehensive about the possibility.

"No. No, sweetheart. I'm just curious if it's the same man."

"Oh." There was a pause. "Do you want me to do it now?"

"Yes." The big man was looking down at his lunch as though seeing it for the first time. He seemed uncomfortable. Something told Megan he was as aware of her as she was of him. "Don't stare," she instructed. "Just take a look and see if you think you recognize him."

"Okay." She heard P.J. suck in his breath the way he did before he jumped into the swimming pool. He turned his head very, very slowly, as though he were afraid it would come off if he moved too quickly. Several seconds passed. He turned back, his expression serious. "Yeah," he whispered.

"Yeah, what?"

"I think it's him. I think it's the guy from the bear cage. I'm pretty sure. What are we gonna do?"

Good question, Megan thought. "Nothing," she said, giving him a smile. "We're going to finish our lunch."

"But—do you think maybe he's following us? He could be a kidnapper or something! I've seen all about stuff like that on TV—"

"It's nothing like that, P.J.," she assured him firmly. "It's probably just a coincidence."

"Is that good or bad?"

"Neither. Now, finish up your hamburger before it gets cold."

"Can I look at him to make really, really sure?"

"No. It's not nice to stare at people."

Afterward, Megan admitted she probably overreacted to the situation. But, given the string of circumstances, overreaction seemed almost inevitable.

She and P.J. finished their lunch and dumped their trash into a waste receptacle.

"Megan," P.J. said in an uneasy voice, "that guy is getting up, too."

"It's all right," she replied, taking him by the hand. Normally, he would have objected to such a show of protectiveness. Now his small fingers gripped hers gratefully.

They exited the restaurant and headed across the parking lot to where she'd left the car. On the day after she'd moved into the beach house, Swann had casually tossed her the keys to his black Ferrari and told her to use the expensive sports car whenever she needed it.

"Megan, he's *following* us!"

Megan had the car keys out. Inserting them deftly into the lock, she opened the door. "It's all right," she repeated. "Just get in the car."

Perhaps if the man hadn't reached for P.J.. Perhaps if P. J. hadn't let out such an alarmed yelp. Then, maybe, what happened next wouldn't have happened. But the man did reach out and P.J. did yelp. From that point on, all Megan's responses were automatic and highly professional.

The big man was right behind her, his right arm extended. Grabbing his wrist with her left hand, she stepped into him with her right foot and started to pivot. Her right shoulder connected solidly with his armpit.

It was a basic judo throw, one of the first she'd learned. The man was caught unprepared. It was a simple matter to use his own momentum and weight against him. He went down gracelessly and landed like a sack of potatoes, his exclamation of surprised protest turning into an explosive release of breath.

Megan bundled P.J. into the car and hit the horn of the car with the heel of her hand.

Thirty seconds later, they were surrounded by a small crowd. Thirty seconds after that, two uniformed policemen, who'd been on line inside the restaurant, came dashing up.

"Okay, okay," the senior of the two officers said authoritatively. "What's going on here?"

After fifteen chaotic and confusing minutes, Megan was asking the same question. But her tone of inquiry wasn't nearly as reasonable as the officer's had been.

Four pieces of information had emerged about the man she'd flipped onto the parking lot pavement. Five pieces, if you counted his assertion that he'd thrown out his back when he'd landed on the asphalt.

First, the man was armed. He made no protest when the policemen swiftly relieved him of the serviceable .38 Smith and Wesson he had tucked in a hip holster.

Second, he said his name was Lewis Bosley.

Third, he carried a private investigator's license.

And fourth, he claimed he worked for Colin Swann.

"And you say you work for Colin Swann, too?" the senior officer asked Megan. His partner had Lewis Bosley, P.I., on his feet and handcuffed. Bosley looked very unhappy.

"Megan takes care of me," P.J. piped up. "Colin Swann is my Daddy. I'm P.J."

"Do you know this Mr. Bosley, son?"

"Officer, I told you—" Bosley began to say.

"I don't think that's necessary—" Megan interrupted.

"He was at the zoo with the bears," P.J. said helpfully. "Megan asked me if I recognized him. So I looked real carefully, and I did."

"But, do you *know* him?" the policeman asked. He clearly hadn't had much experience interrogating six-year-olds.

"He chased us and he tried to grab Megan—"

"Kid, I did not try to grab—"

"Yes, sir! I saw! Only Megan throwed you on the ground!"

"P.J., it's okay," Megan said quickly, squatting down to his level and taking both his hands in hers. She looked at the policeman. "Officers, can't we get this straightened out somewhere a little more *private?*"

The cops exchanged quick glances. "Yes, ma'am," the senior one agreed. "I think we'd all better go down to the station."

P.J.'s eyes grew large. He leaned into Megan, dropping his voice to a whisper. "Are we getting arrested?" he asked.

"Daddy! Daddy!" P.J. hollered when Swann made his explosive entrance at the police station. He moved with the swift, dangerous grace of a black panther, his manner imperious and implacable.

Bernie McGillis followed in his dynamic wake as did Megan's brother, Kyle, resplendent in his chauffeur's uniform. Megan barely registered their presence. Swann drew her eyes like a magnet draws metal filings.

He checked his long strides as he heard P.J.'s voice, the anger and anxiety in his arrestingly handsome face turning to relief. He scooped his son into his arms as the little boy ran to him.

P.J. went into the hug chattering like a tape recorder on fast-forward. His excited account of what had happened was disjointed and barely comprehensible. But the words *Megan* and *big bad guy* came through loud and clear.

Silver-gray eyes met hazel ones over P.J.'s dark head. Megan realized that some of the anxiety—and the relief—she had read printed on Swann's features had been for her For a few mind-spinning seconds, his gaze was utterly open to her. The tenderness of it enveloped her like an embrace.

"You should've seen, Daddy! It was like that stuff you learned in Japan. Megan beat him up. It was *great!*"

And then Swann's expression changed again. Relief gave way to comprehension and some of the anger returned.

"Bosley, what the *hell* is going on here?" he demanded, his eyes fixed on a point behind Megan, stabbing like fencing foils.

"You know him?"

The question came simultaneously from three different sources: Bernie McGillis, the senior police officer, and Megan.

Swann nodded once. "Yes I know him. His name is Lewis Bosley and he's a private detective. I hired him as a bodyguard for my son."

"I cannot believe you did this, Swann," Megan burst out furiously eight hours later. Out of concern for P.J., she'd kept a check on her tongue following his father's revelation at the police station. But now the little boy was safely tucked in bed, soothed and sung to sleep, and she was ready to let fly. Under normal circumstances, she probably would have cooled off by this point. Megan's temper tended to flash hot and fast—long simmering burns were not her style. But these were not normal circumstances.

Dammit, *nothing* in her life had been normal since she'd met Colin Swann!

They were in the gadget-crammed room where Swann holed up when he was working at home. He was leaning against the closed door, his arms folded across his chest. She was pacing. She felt confused, hurt, and angry. She wanted to kick something.

The room, which even P.J. was prohibited from entering without his father's permission, was quite small. Its modest dimensions were strained by the tens of thousands of dollars' worth of audio equipment it contained. The room was also soundproof, which probably was why Swann had led Megan in there and shut the door after they'd put P.J. to bed.

"I really can't believe it," she repeated. "You hired me to take care of your son. I thought you *trusted* me!"

"Megan—"

"Good Lord, Swann, do you have any idea what was going through my head at McDonald's? And when an armed man grabs you—"

"Bosley explained why he came after you and P.J."

She glared at him. "Oh, yes. He realized we'd spotted him and he decided he'd better tell us who he was and what he was doing before we got—what was his phrase?—bent out of shape." She quoted the private detective with acid emphasis.

"All right." Swann held up a placating hand. "Bosley handled the situation badly. And he was the one who—ah—got bent out of shape."

"It's not funny!"

"I'm not saying it is. I told him he had to be discreet after the business at the zoo—"

"Discreet? How can a man the size of one of the Rocky Mountains be discreet?"

"Look, you never noticed him before—"

"Wrong!" she exploded without thinking. "I've been watching him pound sand on the beach every morning for—" She's stopped, flushing bright pink.

"You've been watching *him?"* Swann echoed, the words coming out as taut as a tightrope. His silver-gray eyes were sharp as scissors, ready to slash through whatever she might say next.

"I—" Oh, Lord. All of a sudden, she was in the middle of a minefield. Most of the mines were ones she'd laid;

only she couldn't remember exactly where they were. One wrong step and *ka-blooey!* "He—I caught sight of him one day while I was looking at the pool. He is hard to overlook."

"You didn't say anything."

She swallowed. "I—was there some reason I should've?" she countered, lifting her chin. She reminded herself that she wasn't supposed to know anything about the letters threatening Swann's life. As Megan Louise Harper, nanny-for-hire, she wasn't supposed to have any reason to be suspicious of Mack truck-sized men who jogged up and down on the beach.

"Megan—" He straightened up, pushing away from the door.

"Why didn't *you* say anything when P.J. mentioned the man by the bear cage?" she asked. The calculated dishonesty—*the deliberate duplicity*—of the way she was acting was starting to make her feel a little sick. But she didn't know what else to do. Maybe this was what her father meant by getting dug in when working undercover. If it was, Megan wondered how anyone could stand it. It was like being buried alive.

Swann sighed a long, drawn-out exhalation of breath. He rubbed the back of his neck. "You're right," he said after a moment of silence. "I'm sorry."

Megan stopped pacing. "W-what?" It was the last thing in the world she'd expected.

"I'm sorry," he repeated quietly. "Look, will you sit down and let me try to explain? Bernie McGillis accuses me of thinking I'm the Lone Ranger at times and this is—" He gestured. "Please, Megan, sit down."

After a second or two, she did as he requested, sitting down in the only chair in the room that wasn't piled with sheet music or albums or cassettes. Her movements were slow, almost reluctant. He was going to open up to her, tell her the truth.

She felt awful.

Swann cleared another chair with the careless sweep of his hand. He turned it around and straddled it. "Okay..." He ran his long-fingered hands through his hair several times and then regarded Megan levelly. "For the past few months, I've been getting crank letters."

"Crank? You mean threatening?"

His mouth twisted. "Well, they're not fan letters," he replied. "They're unsigned. But they all apparently come from the same person."

"Do you have any idea—?"

"No." He shook his head. He didn't seem to find anything unusual about her questions. From a professional point of view, Megan knew she had to probe. From the personal side...

Admit it, Megan, she thought. You're concerned, worried, *scared*—and it doesn't have a damn thing to do with business.

"So far, the letters have only been directed at me," he went on. "There's been no reference to my son or anyone else. But I've been—while P.J. was at my mother's, I didn't have to worry about anyone getting close to him. Once he moved in here..."

"You hired Lewis Bosley to be his bodyguard."

"And yours."

She didn't hide her surprise. *"Mine?"*

He nodded. "Yeah. But if the way he was eyeing you at the zoo is anything to go by, Bosley would like to do more than *guard* your body."

Megan felt her cheeks grow hot. "I think he might like to *break* my body after the scene in the McDonald's parking lot," she said.

"You did do quite a bit of damage to his professional ego," Swann conceded. "Speaking of which... I didn't realize nannies came equipped with a working knowledge of karate." He gave the last word a faintly foreign inflection. It was the same inflection Kyle used, and Kyle had a black belt.

Megan made a face. "P.J. exaggerated," she said. The little boy's account of what she'd done to Lewis Bosley had become increasingly outrageous each time he'd given it—and he'd given it to anyone and everyone who'd listen. She shuddered to think of the story he'd spin for Joey Guarino tomorrow when the two got together to play. "And it wasn't karate. It was judo."

"Ah." The sound was neutral. The lift of his arrogant dark brows was emphatically questioning.

Megan laced her fingers together. "I—my father is a retired police officer," she told him carefully. "He's a big believer in women knowing some basic self-defense."

"Just in case saying no doesn't work?"

She knew, looking at him, that he was thinking about what had happened between them out on the couch in the living room. She shifted, feeling the traitorous stirring of her body.

"Why didn't you tell me about Bosley?" she asked.

He let her off the hook . . . this time. "Because I didn't want you to worry. I wasn't certain how you'd react to the idea. And I didn't want P.J. to know."

"I wouldn't have told him!"

"I realize that," he reassured her quickly. "But you might have acted differently if you'd known. And P.J. would have picked up on that." He hesitated, clearly deciding what more he intended to say—and how he intended to say it. "From the time I was nine . . . nearly through the end of high school . . . I had bodyguards. In the beginning, nobody explained. But I knew. At first, I was scared to death. Then, for a little while, it seemed fun—something special. But, over the long haul . . ." He shook his head. "I started to feel so *isolated*. And so alienated. To say nothing of sexually frustrated."

"Sexually—?"

"Ever go out on a date chaperoned by a bodyguard?"

"Oh." She studied her fingers for a few seconds and then looked at him. "All right, I understand about Bosley," she said, "about why you hired a bodyguard for P.J. without telling me. But—what . . . do you have a bodyguard for yourself?" Wouldn't it be the blackest of ironies if, after all her subterfuge—

"No." It was short and definitely unsweet. "I don't need one."

"Why?" she challenged. "Because you know karate?"

He probably was expecting the first question. After all, he'd gone around and around on the subject with his manager. But he was visibly surprised by the second.

"What makes you think I know karate?" he asked sharply.

"The way you say it," she explained. "And P.J. mentioned the stuff you learned in Japan after I threw Mr. Bosley."

"Ah."

There was a pause. Megan worried the inside of her lower lip with her teeth for a few moments. "Swann," she began to say tentatively. "About the letters—"

"Never mind about the letters."

"But if there's a chance that whoever's writing them is serious—"

"Megan, no."

"You don't understand." She desperately wanted him to show some hint of softening on the subject. Just a tiny indication of give on his part, and perhaps she'd be able to find a way to tell him the truth. "If—you've got to take *some* precautions—"

"*No.*" His eyes had gone as opaque as sheet metal. "I don't want a bodyguard. Just leave it alone."

Her heart sank. She left the issue alone.

"What about Lewis Bosley?" she asked finally.

Swann smiled. "After your performance, I think we can dispense with Mr. Bosley's services."

* * *

She couldn't sleep. She tossed. She turned. She plumped and pounded her pillow. She counted sheep—including the ones that looked like Lewis Bosley.

Megan still couldn't sleep.

At twelve minutes to one, she sat up and switched on the small lamp beside her bed. She gazed around the cream, peach and jade room without blinking. The decor, for the most part, was coolly contemporary. Yet there were hints of romanticism here and there—fresh flower arrangements and an old-fashioned chaise longue covered in watered silk. There were touches of whimsy, too, such as the bronze frog that served as a doorstop. The room was feminine without being fussy. It was nothing like Megan's cluttered, comfortable apartment in style, but it had suited her from the very first.

Patti Guarino had told her that Swann had been very specific when he'd picked out the furnishings and color scheme for it.

The softly glowing digital clock on the night table blinked away another minute. Eleven to one.

Ten to one.

Not even a yawn.

Nine to one.

Megan got up. Padding to the chaise, she picked up her robe and pulled it on. It was a simple wrap of distinctive, floral-printed cotton that matched the shortie nightgown and briefs she was wearing. The outfit had been a birthday present from her brother Steve's wife, Lynda.

Tiptoeing down the hall, she checked on P.J. As she expected, Buddy was curled up at the foot of his bed. Smiling a little, Megan stroked a silky lock of hair back from the little boy's forehead. Even in the serenity of sleep, his childish features held a hint of innocent mischief.

The door to Swann's bedroom was firmly shut and

there was no sound from within. Megan closed her mind to the thought of what P.J.'s father looked like when *he* slept.

Of course, Swann knew what *she* looked like . . .

Megan felt herself flush in the darkness.

She went downstairs, intending to get some milk, but the view through the glass doors in the living room captured her attention. It was a flawlessly clear summer night outside. The sky had the velvety richness of a blue-purple pansy and the moon hung against it like a silver Christmas ornament.

A faint breeze ruffled the surface of the moonlight-frosted water in the pool. The whole area had an enchanted and enchanting aura.

Slowly, she undid the lock on the glass door and slid it open.

The glazed tiles on the deck were cool and smooth against her bare feet. The air was fresh and clean with just a tang of salt and sea. It was very quiet . . . very still.

And yet it made her feel very restless. She was aware of a strange sense of expectation . . . anticipation.

She walked to the pool and dipped her toes in. The water was perfect. The reflection of the night sky danced on its rippling surface. Inviting. Enticing.

Why not? she asked herself. You know you want to.

She took off her robe and dropped it on the deck. Just a quick swim, she decided. Something to relax her. She hesitated for a moment, glancing over her shoulder at the darkened house. It, like the night, was very quiet . . . very still.

Temptation, and an odd sort of recklessness, won. Megan's scanty nightgown joined her robe. She kept her briefs on. She stood poised on the edge of pool for several moments. A heady, almost fierce sense of freedom filled her.

She dived in.

The water welcomed her . . . and she welcomed it.

She had no idea how long she swam and played. Seconds. Minutes. Hours. They seemed to have lost their meaning for her. Time was either moving at an incredibly rapid pace, or it was standing entirely still.

And then, suddenly, she knew she wasn't alone.

She stood up, clearing her face of her hair with a snap of her head. She blinked away the drops of water that beaded her long lashes as she focused, trembling, on the tall, dark, emphatically male figure standing at the end of the pool by her discarded pile of nightclothes.

Swann. She knew her lips moved to form his name, but she wasn't certain if she said it aloud. She wasn't certain if she *could* say it aloud.

The water wasn't that deep where she was. Except for the silvery rivulets dripping down over her from her sodden curls, she was naked from the waist up. Instinct brought her arms up and crossed them in front of her full, bared breasts.

He was wearing a short, dark robe that left most of his long, leanly muscled legs uncovered. His feet were planted slightly apart as though he needed to brace himself for balance. His arms were at his sides. There was tension in every line of his posture and his hands were clenched into fists.

Perhaps he said her name; she wasn't sure. She watched, eyes wide and pulse pounding, as he undid the belt of his robe with ritual deliberation and shrugged out of the garment.

He was naked. The moonlight embraced his body, celebrating its fluid symmetry and strength. There was pride and passion and power in the set of his head and shoulders . . . the tapering sculpture of his torso . . . the unashamed thrust of his manhood.

Megan knew without consciously thinking it through that the choice was hers. She could shake her head or turn away. She also knew that she'd already made her choice.

Slowly, even more slowly than she'd brought them up, Megan lowered her arms.

Swann dived into the pool. The water seemed to open for a split second to accept him, barely rippling as he knifed through the surface.

He came up about a foot from her, his black hair plastered to his skull, the water sheeting off his tanned skin. Here and there, drops sparkled in his chest hair. Megan wanted to lick them away. She wanted to hold him . . . caress him . . . to learn his body as intimately as the moonlight had.

Desire was stark on his austere yet sensually carved face. His expression was taut, almost drawn.

He lifted both hands and cupped her face, tilting it up so their eyes met and linked. Megan was a willing captive to his compelling gaze and possessive touch.

Swann traced her slightly angular features one by one, endowing each with a beauty Megan hadn't known it possessed. He found harmony in the spacing of her wide-set eyes, in the not-quite-straight-line of her nose, and unexpected fullness of her lower lip.

"You *are* real," he murmured softly. So softly Megan wasn't sure he intended the words for her ears.

She nodded anyway. "Can you hear my heart beating?" she asked, her voice husky.

His laugh feathered along her nerves. "I can see it," he responded. "Here—" Leaning forward, he pressed his lips against her right temple. His warm breath fanned her skin. "And here . . ."

His mouth slid down, seeking and finding the pulse at the base of her throat. She shuddered with pleasure as she felt the lap of his tongue against her damp skin.

"Swann—" She tilted her head to the side, leaving her neck vulnerable. At the same time, she reached for him.

Her first touch jolted him, telling her more eloquently than words the power she had over him. He made no effort to disguise the effect she'd had.

Physically, he was a stranger to her. Yet the feel of him, the response and heat, was familiar. Somehow—had she absorbed it without realizing through their daily contact? Or through those few kisses they'd shared?—Megan *knew* him. It was not a question of experience or instinct. The knowledge was just there. Complete. Clamoring to be used.

Swann kissed his way back up her throat, the stubbly, new beard growth on his chin rasping faintly against her skin. He took her mouth hungrily, feasting on it, savoring its yielding ripeness. He coaxed her lips apart with delicate, nibbling forays . . . then conquered with one bold thrust of his tongue.

His hands glided down her twisting body at the same time hers came up and locked behind his neck. Her fingers tangled in the thick, wet hair at his nape at the same moment his slipped beneath the elastic of her briefs. She gasped against his lips, arching as she felt his palms curve to shape her buttocks. The cool water lapped against her heated skin in subtle, sensuous insinuation.

His kisses were fiercer now, more demanding. It was as though he couldn't get enough of her. The massaging movements of his hands on the lower part of her body were evocatively insistent. She shuddered, her fingers digging into his scalp in a convulsive reaction, as his caresses became more and more intimate.

Suddenly, he lifted her high and hard against him. Her soft breasts pressed against his chest. She could feel the disordered force of his breathing and the pounding drive of his heart. She clasped her legs around him tightly, aware of the throb of his manhood.

"Megan, love—" Swann's voice was urgent, its velvet richness gone harsh with need. "I have to—"

"Yes. Swann, *please*—" It was permission and a plea. She felt as though she were being enveloped . . . invaded . . . by liquid flames. But the sensation didn't frighten her. Desire unlike anything she'd ever experienced or imagined ignited deep within her, consuming all her inhibitions and uncertainties, leaving her unfettered and completely open.

Swann had maneuvered them to the side of the pool. Megan had been only dimly aware of the ripple and release of his muscles as he'd moved. Now she leaned back, the rounded tile edge supporting her shoulders. She offered herself to him, half surrendering, half seducing.

"You are so beautiful," he told her, covering her breasts with his hands. He molded the full curves with his palms, his fingers wooing the straining, sensitive flesh in a way that was both playful and provocative. He feathered the balls of his thumbs lightly over her nipples ... rotating, rubbing, in smaller and smaller circles, creating a lancing pleasure that arrowed straight to her core. "Your skin is like mother-of-pearl in the moonlight."

She cried out as he bent his dark head and took her right nipple into his mouth, sucking rhythmically on the rose-petal tip until it was taut and aching with arousal. The other breast pouted temptingly, and he finally transferred his erotic attentions to it.

He showed her his greed ... and his generosity. For every pleasure he took—and he treated her body as though it was a banquet created for his private delectation—he gave one in return.

Finally it was no longer a matter of his pleasure or hers. It became impossible to separate them. By then Megan no longer felt consumed by flames—she'd become the fire. She reached for him again and again, the movements of her body frank and frantic against his.

"Megan, look at me," he groaned. One of his hands was questing between her thighs, his fingers demanding yet delicate against the secret places of her womanhood.

She did as he asked, seeing herself reflected in his eyes. The moonlight clung to the planes and hollows of his face like silver leaf.

"I watched you from my window tonight," he whispered. "At first I was afraid you weren't—Lord knows, I've fantasized—"

"I'm . . . real," she said. She wanted him inside her, filling her. To be this close and lack that—"How . . . long—?"

She didn't know whether she was asking him how long he'd watched . . . or fantasized . . . or how long he was going to delay the moment they were both desperate for. She rocked against him in a rhythm as ancient as the seas.

"Too long." And Swann joined them irrevocably with one sure, deep plunge.

For a moment or so afterward, he remained utterly still, almost as though he didn't dare move. He was hard and bold within the silken clasp of her femininity, pulsing with life and vitality.

Then, slowly, with infinite care, he began to thrust. Megan arched herself to meet him, her body warm, welcoming . . . and finally wanton with the sensations she was experiencing. She embraced him, encircling him with her legs as well as her arms. She said his name over and over again.

Swann silenced her with a kiss.

Passion was a wave . . . building, surging. For a few mindless moments, Megan rode the crest of it, traveling to a place she'd only dreamed of.

Then the wave broke, and she was drowning in a pleasure so intense she was not sure if she would survive it. She clung to Swann for love and life, knowing that she was not alone . . . and then ecstasy overwhelmed her.

CHAPTER SIX

WHEN MEGAN AWOKE, she was in her own bed and she was alone.

For a few moments, she was almost as disoriented as she had been that first morning when she'd woken up next to Swann after a night she couldn't remember. Then everything slipped into place.

She recalled Swann's carrying her upstairs after they'd made love in the pool . . . and again in the cabana on the deck. They'd made love a third time—slowly, lingeringly—in her bed before drifting off to sleep in each other's arms. Her soft body had curved against his hard one. His arms had encircled her, and his breath had stirred her hair as he nuzzled tenderly against her neck, whispering.

She didn't remember his leaving her. . . .

Megan sat up slowly, gathering the disordered bedclothes around her in a languid movement. She was naked. She thought she could detect traces of Swann's scent on the sheets . . . and her skin.

The pillow next to her still bore the faint imprint of his head. There was also a folded piece of paper addressed to her sitting on top of it. Megan picked it up, her heart beating a curious tattoo.

While Swann's autograph was a practiced, flamboyant scrawl, his everyday handwriting had an angular spareness to it. The words she read now flowed across the paper with bold simplicity:

Megan:

You're a beautiful woman to wake up with and a hard lady to leave. P.J.'s with me.

Yours, Swann.

After she finished scanning it, Megan stared at the note for nearly a minute, emotions going off inside her like fireworks.

You have to tell him the truth now, a small voice inside her said. You *have* to. After last night, he'll understand.

But what if he doesn't? a second voice demanded. What if he turns you away? He still needs protection. *Your* protection.

Yours, Swann. What does *that* mean?

What did she want it to mean?

She folded and refolded the note. Glancing at the bedside clock, she got a jolt. It was nearly twelve o'clock! She never slept this late.

Throwing back the sheets, she got out of bed. She was still holding Swann's note. After a moment's hesitation, she tucked it underneath the clock.

She needed time.

She showered, her awareness of her own sexuality acute as she soaped and rinsed herself. Swann had been an inventive, experienced lover, and he had taken an uninhibited delight in every detail of her body. His appreciation—demonstrated over and over again with word and touch—had excited her almost beyond the point of reason . . . certainly beyond the point of restraint.

She was conscious of a certain tenderness between her thighs and of faint, fingerprint-shaped bruises on her upper arms. There were physical sensations . . . some new, some simply unfamiliar after more than a year without a man.

Lord, had they really—*in the swimming pool?* And, afterward in the cabana, had she been the one to—?

Flushing, she stepped out of the shower and reached for a towel. She also seemed to remember some discussion of black satin sheets.

She stared at her reflection in the mirror over the sink for a few seconds. There were the same thirty-year-old features she'd seen the morning before. And yet—

There was a new, bruised softness to her mouth. And there was a more knowing look in her hazel eyes . . . as well as a hint of vulnerability.

What was it Swann had said to her? *You can't avoid the inevitable. And you can't hurry what's never going to happen.*

Time. Yes . . . she needed that.

She dried herself off, quickly scrubbed her teeth, and then dressed, pulling on a pair of yellow shorts and a yellow and white patterned top. Grabbing her hairbrush, she tugged it through her tangled curls. After about a dozen strokes, she tossed the brush aside and went downstairs.

She found P.J. sprawled on his stomach in the middle of the living room, surrounded by his collection of plastic "action figures" of characters from Saturday morning cartoons. Buddy was lying on the floor close to him, his tail wagging back and forth.

"Zzz-zzz-zzz—" P.J. imitated the buzz of a ray gun

and then knocked over one of the figures with his finger. "See, Buddy, we got the bad—" He broke off, looking up. "Hey, Megan!" The youngster scrambled to his feet. "Daddy, Megan's up!" he called in the direction of Swann's room. Glancing that way, Megan saw that the door to the room was partially open.

"Morning, P.J.," she said, turning her attention back to the little boy. "Good morning to you, too, Buddy."

"Not *morning*," P.J. corrected with a giggle. Buddy yipped. "It's almost lunchtime! Daddy's going to let me make baloney and cheese sandwiches. Do you want one?"

"Give Megan a break, Peej," Swann suggested lightly, coming into the living room with his usual noiseless tread. He was wearing nothing but a pair of denim cut-offs and a Nightshade T-shirt that had been faded to near-illegibility by repeated washings. "She just got up. I think she might prefer black coffee to baloney."

For a moment, everything stood still. There was just the two of them in the room . . . in the world. Megan hadn't known what the first meeting with her lover of one night would bring. She'd braced herself for embarrassment, awkwardness—even indifference. Instead, she felt a little shy for the first few seconds. Then, that shyness dissolved in a hot, sweet surge of emotion.

Their eyes met. It only lasted an instant. But in that instant, Megan knew: For her, Colin Swann was the inevitable.

"Good morning," he greeted her softly. He smiled.

"Good morning." She returned the words and the smile.

"Did you sleep good?" P.J. asked. "Me and Buddy did."

"Uh—yes." Megan's eyes went from Swann to his son and back again. She lifted one hand and patted her hair, the silken texture of it pleasant against her fingers.

"You were really tired, huh? Daddy said you were. How come? Was it from beating up Mr. Bosley?"

"P.J.—" Megan began to say.

"P.J., I thought we went through this and agreed that Megan didn't beat up Mr. Bosley," Swann cut in.

The little boy pulled a face. "Yeah. But she *could've*," he insisted. "I bet Joey thinks—oh!" His expression brightened and he turned a grin on Megan. "Hey, Megan. Guess what! I'm staying at Joey's tonight!"

"You are?" She and Patti had arranged for the two boys to get together that afternoon, but nothing had been said about sleeping over.

P.J. nodded. "Yeah. Daddy asked his mom."

Hazel eyes collided with silver-gray ones. "What a surprise," Megan said.

She wasn't sure what she was feeling. Anger, perhaps, at the assumptions Swann obviously had made. Anxiety, possibly, too. And anticipation. Yes, blossoming in the midst of all her other unsettled emotions, there was a definite sense of anticipation as well.

"Yeah," P.J. said innocently, "I didn't know anything about it till Daddy said."

"And now Daddy says it'd be a good idea for you to scoot upstairs and figure out what you want to take over to Joey's," Swann informed him.

"What about lunch?"

"You can have lunch afterward."

"Can I bring Buddy and Godzilla—"

"No." Megan and Swann spoke simultaneously.

P.J.'s eyes went back and forth between them. "You guys are weird sometimes," he announced obscurely and then marched upstairs.

"So . . ." Swann said, crossing to her with lithe, leisurely strides. He stopped about a foot away from her. Megan had to lift her chin to look up into his eyes. "My son thinks we're weird."

She swallowed. "Only sometimes." She remembered digging her fingers into his shoulders the night before, at the height of her passion. His muscles had been taut, unyielding, but she had clasped him, claimed him, with wanton strength. She wondered suddenly if his body bore the marks of her nails.

A sensual smokiness swirled through his eyes. "I'm not sure I want to know what he thinks of us the rest of the time'," he responded huskily.

He kissed her. Once on the left corner of her mouth, once on the right. Then his tongue traced the full curve of her lower lip, and she began to kiss him back.

All in all, the kiss was more playful than provocative. His mouth was firm yet flirtatious; hers was tender yet tantalizing. The question of who was taking, who was giving, was unanswerable and unnecessary.

It was impossible to say who ended the caress. It seemed to happen by mutual consent. When they broke apart, Megan knew that Swann's breathing was as unsteady as her own.

His hands lingered briefly on the sides of her breasts as though recording their responsive fullness. Megan hadn't bothered with a bra this morning. She could feel her nipples, unrestrained and aroused, go stiff against the stretchy cotton knit of her top.

"I meant what I wrote," he told her quietly, letting his hands drop away. "About your being a beautiful woman to wake up with and a hard lady to leave."

She knew she must be blushing, but her whole body felt so warm and melting, she couldn't be certain.

"But—" his eyes slid to the stairs, his brows going up. "I thought, all things considered, you'd prefer to wake up in your own bed . . . alone."

Obviously, it was a reference to P.J. But Megan thought she detected a deeper attunement to her other misgivings as well. "All things considered," she said, "thank you."

"You're welcome."

She shifted, glancing away from him. *Yours, Swann.* Did he mean that, too?

"Megan?"

She looked at him again. "What did Patti say when you—arranged tonight's sleep-over?"

An amused smile tugged at the corner of his mouth. It was plain he'd expected such a question. "You're absolutely certain it was my idea?" he parried.

"Of cour—" She stopped, recalling the conversation with Patti by the pool. Had Coney's wife gone beyond wondering to matchmaking? "Swann, what did she say?"

"She said, and I quote: 'Well, it's about time.'"

"Dad, it's Megan." It was about ninety minutes later. Swann was driving P.J. to the Guarino house and then going on to an interview. He'd asked Megan to dinner that night. She'd agreed. "I'm sorry I didn't call last night. But things got—"

"That's okay. Kyle explained what happened. Sounds like you cleaned Bosley's clock."

"Little P.J. keeps insisting I beat him up. All I did was throw the guy in the middle of McDonald's parking lot." She laughed humorlessly. "Which was probably quite enough."

"Swann's suspicious?" Simon Harper asked sharply.

"No," Megan answered quickly. "At least, he doesn't seem to be. I told him my father was a retired police officer who believes in women knowing self-defense."

"The truth but not the whole truth. That's always the best line to walk in this sort of situation," her father said.

"Do you know this Lewis Bosley?" Megan questioned, trying not to think about 'this sort of situation.' She wasn't walking the line anymore; she'd crossed it.

"I know his reputation. It's solid. Swann may have a beef against security people, but he hired himself a topnotch man. Of course, he didn't know he already had a topnotch woman—"

"Right, Dad," she interrupted, not wanting to hear that particular point underscored. "Incidentally, do you know if Bosley is okay? He seemed a little hunched over when I last saw him." She had visions of a massive disability suit.

"Well, from what I hear, he may be laid up for a week or so."

"Seriously?"

"He's got a trick back. But, don't worry. You didn't do permanent damage. Except maybe to his ego. I don't imagine a big macho guy like Bosley likes the idea of getting taken by a woman."

"Probably not," Megan said.

There was a brief pause. "Ah—Kyle says it got a little hairy with Swann yesterday at the police station."

"He was worried about his son. Can you blame him?"

"Kyle had the impression he was worried about *you,* too."

"Yes, well, you know how impressionable Kyle can be."

There was another pause. A much longer one this time. Megan began chewing the inside of her lip.

"Is there something going on you want to tell me about?" her father inquired slowly.

Megan didn't say anything. *You have the right to remain silent,* she thought to herself.

"Megan?" The use of her full first name was a bad sign.

Anything you say can and will be held against you.

"Meg, is there something—"

"No."

"No, there's nothing going on . . . or no, you don't want to tell me about it?"

"Dad—"

"You're part of a case, a *key* part."

"I know that."

"Do you?"

"Yes!"

"Sweetheart—"

"Dad, please. I'm thirty years old. I'm a professional. I know what I'm doing."

"I don't want you to get hurt."

"Are you speaking as my father or my boss?" She regretted the question almost as soon as she uttered it. "Dad—"

"Meg, there was another letter this morning."

She gripped the phone so hard her knuckles went white. *"Another* one? So soon?"

"Yeah. Another L.A. postmark. It's uglier than the one before. There's a line about when the music stops for good. And there was a photograph with a bull's-eye drawn on it."

"Dear Lord."

"Meg, it wasn't any PR or magazine picture. It's a telephoto lens job. Kyle looked at it and said he thinks it must've been taken last week when Swann was on his way to the recording studio."

Meg forced herself to breathe in and out for several seconds, fighting a sense of dread. "Then this isn't just some nut sending letters anymore," she said. "He . . . he's following Swann." *I'm coming for you,* she remembered the threat.

"That's what it looks like. There's one other thing. The number five was printed in the middle of the bull's-eye."

"Five?"

"Yeah. Does that mean something to you?"

She frowned. "No . . ." she said slowly, "I don't think so."

"Swann's never mentioned the number five?"

"Not that I remember." She searched her memory but came up blank. "Dad, it could be anything. A date. An hour. Some sort of crazy code. *Anything.*"

"Then again, it could be nothing."

"The agency hasn't had any luck tracing the letters?"

"We're working on it. Look, I want you to be extra

careful from now on, do you hear me?"

"I will be, Dad," she promised.

"And, Meg—"

"Yes?"

"That last bit was me speaking as your father."

"Are you having second thoughts about last night?" Swann asked softly, watching Megan from across the table.

Megan toyed with her fork for a moment, not certain how she wanted to answer—or *if* she wanted to answer. Their conversation to this point had been friendly and more than a little flirtatious, but there had been an undercurrent of intimacy flowing beneath all their exchanges. Now, obviously, Swann wanted to bring that undercurrent to the surface.

"Yes, I've been having second thoughts," she admitted, staring down at the remains of her chocolate mousse. "And third and fourth and fifth ones." She looked up at him. "I—I've been thinking about last night."

"So have I." He sat back, but he didn't relax.

They were lingering over coffee and dessert in a restuarant called Le Chardonnay. Swann's choice of place had surprised her a little. She had expected him to opt for a trendy spot like Spago's, which served pizza and pasta to a flashy parade of celebrities, or an elegant establishment like Ma Maison, where Hollywood society dined on the *hautest* of *cuisine*. While Megan had never been to either, she'd read about them, and she assumed that Swann had more than a passing familiarity with both.

Yet, instead of those restaurants, he'd brought her to this whimsically romantic place that definitely was more in the spirit of the Boulevard Saint-Germain than Beverly Hills. The setting—huge, arched mirrors, floral-carved rosewood paneling, and nostalgic, amber-toned lighting from lovely frosted fixtures—evoked Paris during La Belle Epoque. The food—rich terrines, grilled fish, and spit-roasted meats and poultry——was bistro-style at its best. Megan had liked Le Chardonnay the moment she'd set foot in it.

She *didn't* like the way Swann was looking at her. Or perhaps she liked it too much. The eyes she had once thought shut her out were now drawing her in . . . embracing her . . . absorbing her.

Swann's gaze was like his kiss: an act of utter concentration.

"All right." He made a placating gesture. In his gray linen suit, white silk shirt, and black and silver tie, he looked like the definition of the word *debonair*. The impeccable style of his clothes was European and expensive, yet he wore the garments with the same sexy, casual panache he wore his jeans. "Tell me about your second thoughts."

She steepled her fingers. "They're the same ones I had before last night."

"You think that this—that *we're* a mistake."

"I—" How could she call the ecstasy, the fulfillment, they had shared a mistake? "Swann, I'm not bla—"

She stopped, realizing she was on the verge of saying she didn't blame him. Lord, if there was any blame to be handed out in this situation, it should go to her! She was a responsible, adult woman. She'd known what she was doing. And Swann had been honest about his intentions—

Honest. She flinched away from the word. Tell him, Megan Louise, a little voice urged.

"Megan?"

She met his questioning eyes. "I—I've been thinking about those letters you've been getting, too."

"No," he said, "I don't want you to think about those."

"But—"

Leaning forward, he reached across the table and took one of her hands. "Megan, I told you about those letters because I wanted to explain why I hired Lewis Bosley.

I didn't tell you to worry you—or frighten you."

"Maybe I'm frightened for *you!*"

"Don't be," came the implacable reply. "I can take care of myself."

"Why are you so stubborn about this?"

An odd, humorless smile twisted the corner of his mouth. "Because that's the way I am." The words were flat and uncompromising.

Megan let a few seconds pass and then tried another tack. "Your manager knows about these letters, doesn't he?" she asked.

Swann released her hand, stroking his fingers down the slender length of hers as he did. "Bernie? Yes. I take it you must have heard some of that song and dance he was performing at the police station."

She nodded slowly. "He seemed worried—"

"He has an investment in me," Swann replied with a tinge of cynicism. "Besides, he's a big believer in the principle of Bernie knows best."

Megan decided to take a risk. "What—what would you do if he hired some security people for you? I mean, the way you hired Lewis Bosley—"

"You mean, what would I do if he went behind my back?" Swann rephrased bluntly.

"Yes." She tried to keep her anxiety out of her voice and off her face. She thought she succeeded. Swann obviously didn't like talking about this, but he didn't seem suspicious of her questions.

"Bernie knows me too well to do anything like that."

The answer and the way it was spoken chilled her. She recalled the manager's remark about Swann's nailing him to the wall if he discovered his deception. She'd thought—hoped, really—that he'd been exaggerating. Suddenly, she didn't think so.

"Megan, why do you think last night happened?" Swann asked abruptly.

"Why?" How in heaven's name was she supposed to answer that?

"Yes. *Why?*"

"I—two people in the same house—" she floundered.

"Proximity? Look, contrary to popular opinion, I do not bed every female within reach," he cut in. "At least . . . not anymore."

Megan swallowed, wondering at the hint of pain she detected in his tone. "I know that," she told him softly, truthfully. She also knew with absolute certainty that if he *did* she wouldn't have made love with him the night before—no matter how much her body might have clamored for it. She'd been one of many with Doug Carlyle; it was not an experience she wanted to repeat.

The tension in his expression eased. "I lived through nearly two years of proximity with Edwina Lynton and I never laid a hand on her," he said wryly.

Megan laughed briefly. "From what I've heard about her, you probably would have lost it if you had."

He laughed, too, and then grew thoughtful. "What was your husband like?" he questioned without warning.

She stiffened. The inquiry might sound like an abrupt change of subject, but she knew it wasn't. "I . . . this has nothing to do with Doug," she replied after a moment.

"I've found the past has a lot to do with the present," he returned. "And the future." She had the feeling he wasn't just talking about her former marriage. "His name was Doug?"

"Carlyle," she answered reluctantly. "He—you're nothing like him."

"God, I hope not! I'd hate to think I have anything in common with a first-class fool."

"A fool?" Doug had been clever. Ve
cleverness—and her own refusal to acce
had been one reason their marriage had g
long as it had.

"Any man who had you and let you go fits my definition of a fool—or worse."

Megan glanced away, shaken by what she thought she saw in the depths of his eyes. "I—he didn't let me go," she confessed. "I left him."

"Why?"

"He—there were a lot of reasons." There had been four specific reasons that she'd found out about. Lord only knew how many others there might have been.

"He cheated." There was contempt in Swann's voice.

Her gaze sliced back to him. "Yes," she admitted.

"But you were faithful to him."

"Yes!"

"Megan—" Swann leaned forward. "It wasn't a question." He paused for a moment. "Did you meet him through your work?"

"Doug's a lawyer. I—I met him through one of my brothers." That was true. Kyle *had* been the one who'd introduced her to Doug when he'd come to Harper Security one day to discuss a case.

"Have either of your brothers followed in your father's footsteps?" Swann wanted to know. "Become cops, I mean."

Megan clenched her hands together under the table. She'd known the day was going to come when Swann would want to know more about her. She didn't want to lie, but she knew she had to. As her father had pointed out, she was key to the agency's plan for protecting Colin Swann. And it was becoming clearer that he did need protection.

"My older brother is in electronics," she said, once again taking a cue from her father's counsel about telling the truth but not the whole truth in this kind of situation. "And my younger one is an actor."

"He's in show business?" Swann seemed surprised. "Would I have seen him in anything?"

Megan had to fight down an appalling desire to laugh

at the irony of the question. Would he have seen——? Oh, Lord, yes! He'd had seen Kyle nearly every day——in Swann's own limousine!

"Probably not," she replied. "He'd only done small character parts. He . . . he tends to blend in with the background. But he's very good," she added with a touch of sisterly pride.

"Mmm."

She stared at Swann, feeling her insides unravel like a row of knitting. She had to get him off the subject of her family. "I . . . what was your——what was Iris Ames like?" she blurted out.

For a moment, she thought he was going to refuse to answer. The closing up of his features was unmistakable. She could practically hear the barriers slamming into place.

"Hasn't Patti filled you in on all the details?"

"Patti?" She could feel her cheeks color again. "I—— well, she and I——"

"You've talked," he finished evenly. "It's all right, Megan. I know Patti gossips. I also know she only does it with people she trusts." His sensual mouth twisted. "She wouldn't give Iris the time of day."

"I'm sorry, Swann." Megan wasn't certain what she was apologizing for; she just knew she had to say something.

He shook his head slowly. There were a few moments of silence. When he finally began to speak, his eyes were still shuttered, but his tone was frank.

"Iris was like one of those fake Christmas presents you see in store windows," he said. "Gorgeous wrapping on the outside. Empty on the inside. But I suppose I was a little empty, too, when I met her. It was backstage at a friend's concert. She was waiting for somebody—— something. We had an affair. She got pregnant. I asked her to marry me, but she said no. So, we moved in together. It . . . it lasted about four years. Then, one day, she left for good. She didn't want me. She certainly didn't want P.J. I don't think she knew what she wanted. A year later, she was dead. Except for the needle marks on her arms, she was still gorgeous." He paused, crumpling his napkin. "I was faithful to Iris while we were together. After she walked out . . . I went through six months I'd rather not remember too clearly."

"And then?" Megan prompted very softly.

"And then I woke up one morning and realized I was in danger of screwing up the one good thing that had come out of the mess Iris and I had made."

"P.J."

He nodded. "So, I started to put my act back together. About that time, Bobby Donovan—the lead guitarist for Fallen Angel—died in a boating accident. I stepped in to help the band. Out of that came Nightshade. A real rock-and-roll family."

"You enjoy what you do." Megan was a true Nightshade fan. She knew Swann had tremendous talent. She'd also begun to learn about the integrity and intensity he brought to what he did.

"I enjoy making music. I'm good at it. And I'm good at putting on a show for people. But I don't want to do it forever. There comes a time when either the legs or the larynz start to go. I plan to be out of performing and into producing before that happens. I can't save myself from middle age, but I can spare audiences the sight of a balding, paunchy, over-the-hill rock star trying to hang on to his lost youth."

Megan had to smile. "Somehow, I don't think you'll ever be balding or paunchy."

He smiled back. "No? Do you want to stick around to make sure?"

He asked the question teasingly, but the look in his eyes was anything but casual. Megan's breath thickened and dammed in her throat. "Swann—" It was half protest, half plea.

The look vanished like smoke before a strong wind. "I know. I said I wouldn't rush you."

"I—" He'd also said that they both knew he probably *could* rush her. "What—what about P.J. in all this?" she asked.

An expression she couldn't quite read flickered across Swann's face. "If you want me to ask for his approval, I'm sure he'll give it."

"I don't want him to get hurt," she tried to explain.

"Neither do I." There was a measured, measuring silence. "Megan, it's just the two of us tonight," Swann said at last. "Tell me what you want."

Perhaps it was the burden of her deception that made her absolutely honest with him—and herself—at this point. Perhaps it was that the feelings Swann evoked in her were too strong to be denied. "I want the same thing you want," she answered, and she didn't blush.

CHAPTER SEVEN

"AM I TOO heavy for you?" Swann murmured five nights later, nuzzling her ear gently.

"Nuh . . ." Megan shook her head languidly, her verbal response more a purr of contentment than an actual word. She got a brief hint of bristled chin against her cheek. A delicious shiver ran through her.

P.J. was staying overnight with his Grandma Sandra. Megan and Swann had spent the evening at a small club in West Hollywood where a musician friend of Swann's was trying out some new material and a change of image.

She'd thoroughly enjoyed the experience. The only flaw had been the gimlet-eyed glare her brother Kyle had given her as he'd handed her in and out of the limousine. His expression had made her feel very self-conscious—so self-conscious that she'd behaved like a skittish sixteen-year-old when Swann had taken her into his arms in the back seat of the car on the way back to Malibu. Fortunately, Swann had seemed more amused than anything else by her reticence.

"Is that a yes, Megan?" He continued his erotic explorations for a few seconds. His mouth was warm and coaxing. His breath fanned her skin. "Or a no?"

"Mmm . . . you're not too heavy," she assured him, shutting her mind to all thoughts of her younger brother. She and Swann were sprawled on the floor of his bedroom, partially wrapped in the black satin sheets Rick, Coney, and Boomer had given him for a housewarming present. Shortly after they'd arrived back at the beach house, she'd made a joking reference about them. One thing had led rapidly to another.

Swann was lying half on top of her. Their legs were tangled together with one of his knees riding intimately between her thighs. Megan relished the feel of his body on hers: the crispness of his body hair, the sweat-dampness of his skin, and the sleek power of his male physique. She sighed and shifted as he ran his palm up her torso and captured one of her breasts. She felt her sensitive flesh nestle into the curve of his palm.

"You know, Rick has a theory about women," Swann commented, his voice low and husky. He lifted his head so that he could look down at her. His silver-gray eyes smoldered. His beautifully carved lips curved into a devilish smile.

Megan gazed up at him. Rick Nichols had been at the club tonight, too, accompanied by a breathy brunette who'd clung to him with the tenacity of Super Glue. Although the rangy, sandy-haired bass player was not Megan's type, she understood why women found him so irresistible.

"Much as I like Rick," she said, weaving her fingers through his hair, "I don't really think I want to hear his theory about women. Any man who nicknames his girl friend Raspberry Ripple—"

"You should have seen the one he had in tow three months ago. She was known as Rocky Road."

"I rest my case."

"Well . . . actually, it's a very *interesting* theory." He did something with his hands that sent some very *interesting* sensations skittering clear down to her toes. "Rick says women are like guitars." He began massaging her breast with a slow, rocking motion. Each time he pressed, she felt an answering contraction in the lower part of her body.

Megan's eyes fluttered shut. She forced them open. "I know I'm going to—um—regret asking this," she said, "but why does he—ah!—say something like that?"

"Because . . ." He drew the word out, tiptoeing his fingers to the peaking crest of her nipple. He skated his nail delicately around the puckering aureole.

"Yes?"

"Because you can't be sure a woman's in tune until you play with—hey—*ouch!*"

Megan had lifted her head just enough so she could nip his neck with her teeth.

"Why, you little witch!" Swann exclaimed, shifting his weight so he could control her movements. "I didn't say I agreed with him."

"You probably do," she returned, squirming a little. "You rock stars are all alike."

"Oh, really? And just how many rock stars have you known, sweetheart?"

"Enough to—*oh!*" She arched as his free hand slipped insinuatingly between their bodies. "Please—"

"Hmm . . . maybe Rick's theory does have *some* validity."

"Swann!" She shuddered as his fingers strummed intimately over her flesh.

"I mean, you *do* seem to be responding like a well-played, well-tuned, extremely sensitive instrument . . ."

She moaned, more than a little frustrated, as he stroked her one last time and then withdrew his hand.

It took her about a minute to collect her wits. By that time, Swann was kissing the side of her neck, nibbling lightly, and drawing lustful patterns on her skin with his tongue.

"Swann—?"

"Mmm? Good Lord, Megan, you taste terrific. You should try yourself."

"No, thanks." She laughed unsteadily. "I *would* like to register one tiny complaint, though."

Breaking off his gourmet tour of her throat and shoulders, Swann lifted his head again. "You said I wasn't too heavy—"

"It's not *you*. It's the floor."

"The floor? It seems fine to me."

"That's because you're not the one flat on your back on it."

"Ahh. Hard, huh?"

"In a word, ye—*Swann!*"

Without warning, he reversed their positions, rolling himself on his back and bringing her over to rest on top of him.

"Better?" he inquired, cupping her bottom.

"We-e-ll—"

"Not so hard?"

She gave him a wicked smile and did a provocative little shimmy with her hips. "I wouldn't exactly say that."

He caught his breath. "Why, Megan Louise Harper!" His grip on her derrière tightened.

"You did ask," she reminded him dulcetly.

"So I did," he conceded.

There was a short silence. Megan combed her fingers through his hair. "Have you ever noticed we seem to make love in . . . um . . . *creative* places?" she asked.

"You mean the pool?"

"And the cabana. And the living room couch. And

the limo—" She tried to withdraw the last word, but it was already out.

"Whoa," Swann interrupted simultaneously, "we made *out* in the limousine tonight, remember? You were worried about embarrassing the chauffeur." He teased one of her red-gold curls. "Despite the fact that he was on one side of a soundproof, opaque panel and we were on the other."

"Oh, yes." Megan mumbled, dipping her head, hoping he wouldn't read anything significant into her sudden blush. Bright, she chided herself, that was really bright. As if Swann didn't think your behavior tonight was weird enough already. Do you want him to start wondering *why* you were so concerned about the chauffeur?

"Incidently, speaking about the chauffeur—"

Her head snapped up. "The . . . the chauffeur?"

"Yes, the chauffeur. You know, the young guy in the uniform who sits in the front and drives while we sit in the back and . . . well, don't do much of anything—"

"Swann—" she swallowed. "I know *who* you mean. It's *what* you mean—"

"I think he has a thing for you."

"You—*what?*"

"Not that I blame him, of course."

Discovering a totally unexpected reservoir of acting talent, Megan simulated a laugh. "What in heaven's name makes you think your chauffeur has a thing for me?"

"Because up until the night we went out to dinner at Le Chardonnay, he and I were getting along just fine. Since then he's been looking at me as though I had some sort of communicable disease."

"I hadn't noticed," she said honestly. "I thought he'd been glaring at *me*."

"You?"

She nodded. "Ah—maybe he has a thing for you?" she suggested outrageously, wanting to find some way off this potentially explosive subject.

Her ploy worked. Swann laughed. "That I doubt. I have the distinct feeling—what's his name? Kyle—likes the ladies. I get the same vibes from him I get from Rick."

"Mmm." While Megan wouldn't exactly put her younger brother in Rick's league, she recognized that there were definite similarities.

There was another pause in the conversation.

"You forgot under the kitchen table," Swann commented at last.

"Under the—"

"You were listing the places we'd made love."

"Oh."

"I don't think I've ever enjoyed a midnight snack more."

"Swann!"

"And your idea about the honey was inspired."

"Well—" She flushed, recalling her lack of inhibitions.

"Of course, the stairs—"

"The stairs were *your* idea!"

"Yes, but you got into the spirit of things. You have a terrific sense of balance."

"Bala—I nearly fell over and broke my neck!"

He frowned. "Hmm, now that I think of it, you did seem a little weak-kneed at one point."

His hands suddenly turned possessive, sliding up her back. "Do I make you dizzy, Megan?" he asked in a deep, urgent tone.

His touch was like a torch, her body like dry tinder. *"Do I?"*

"Yes." He made her dizzy with yearning . . . wanting . . . needing.

"Good," he said thickly, pulling her head down for a searing, hungry kiss, "because you make me feel the same way."

* * *

In an unfamiliar place,
She had the kind of face
I knew I'd seen before.
From clear across the room,
I caught the scent of her perfume
And I had the score—

It was late the next afternoon, and Colin Swann was
threading a sinuous path across the dance floor of a
crowded, smoke-filled club with a predatory stride. His
lips moved in perfect sync with the prerecorded lyrics as
he followed a course that had been mapped out with
choreographic precision.

The crowd he was prowling through was hired—ex-
tras paid by the hour. The smoke was manufactured. The
club itself was genuine, rented for the shooting of Nightshade's latest video. Megan was watching the proceed-
ings from a vantage point that was well out of camera
range.

For the most part, she was relishing the opportunity
to see Swann work. Her only problem stemmed from an
awareness of the speculative looks she'd received since
walking onto the set. Although everyone she'd come into
contact with had been pleasant, she'd overheard several
drawling comments about babysitters. Megan wasn't a
shrinking violet, but she didn't feel particularly comfortable getting caught in the glare of Swann's spotlight,
either.

Swann, on the other hand, seemed perfectly at ease
on center stage. At the moment, he was clad in black
jeans and wore a black leather vest without a shirt. A
silver earring—a performance prop—winked in his right
ear lobe. A faint stubble of beard shadowed the contours
of his chin and cheeks. He was wearing a moody, dangerous expression.

In Megan's opinion, he looked incredibly sexy.

"Cut! Dammit, *cut!*" the director yelled suddenly.

"You, sugarplum! In the purple. Yes, *you!* What do you think we're doing? The sequel to Jane Fonda's Workout? I keep telling you, no sweating! Cool! I want *cool!"*

"Maybe we should try air conditioning?" Swann suggested wryly, running his hand through his disordered hair.

"So, how's the kid?" Bernie McGillis inquired under cover of the laughter that greeted Swann's tension-defusing quip. He had sidled up beside Megan without her knowing it.

"P.J.'s fine," Megan replied. She'd seen Swann's manager several times since the conversation in his office the day after the housewarming party, but they'd always kept their contact to a polite minimum.

"I don't see him around."

"He's at his grandmother's—along with his dog Buddy, of course."

"Convenient," he observed without elaboration.

"Swann invited me to watch today's shooting," she said, hoping she didn't sound as defensive as she suddenly felt.

"Hey, it's okay with me," he told her. "Anything that keeps you close to Swann."

Megan stiffened slightly at the innuendo she thought she detected in the comment. "Mr. McGillis—" she started to say.

"Hey, I'm not criticizing," he interrupted. "I more or less figured you two—well, just as long as you keep in mind you're on the inside because of the somebody on the outside—"

"I know why you hired me," Megan replied tersely.

"There was another letter."

Her stomach clenched like a fist. "The same—"

"Pretty much, yeah. There was another one of those damned amateur photographs with a five and a bull's-eye. It was kind of blurry, like the guy's hand was shaking. But I think it must have been taken when Swann came to my office the other day. And, oh, yeah—after the 'I'm coming for you,' the guy wrote '*soon.*' Underlined."

Megan took a long breath. "Does Swann know?"

Bernie nodded. "But you'd never guess it to look at him, would you?"

Megan glanced across the room toward Swann. He was standing impassively while a makeup artist and hair stylist fussed over him. As though he felt the touch of her gaze, he half turned and gave her a quick smile. She smiled back. "No, you'd never guess," she said with a trace of grimness. Others sweated; Colin Swann stayed cool.

"The only good news today is that there may be a lead on the sender."

Her eyes snapped back to Bernie's face. "A lead?"

"Hasn't your father told you? Your agency's been doing some digging. Very discreetly, of course. Somebody turned up the studio secretary who used to handle Iris Ames's fan mail. She swears she remembers that Iris got a bunch of letters similar to those received by Swann."

"Threats, you mean?"

Bernie shook his head. "No. She remembers them as I-love-you-and-we-should-be-together stuff. But she says they *looked* the same—cheap paper, black Magic Markers, lots of underlining and exclamation points."

Megan frowned. "But this was at least—what?—six years ago?" *Her,* she thought. "Could the 'her' be Iris Ames?"

"I wondered about that, too. The secretary says she remembers so clearly because the letters began coming once a week, like clockwork, right after Iris hit it big with her first movie. I guess they started out pretty normal, but they got wilder and wilder. Then they stopped all of a sudden, after about a year."

"They were unsigned?"

"Yeah. This secretary *thinks* some of them were post-marked Chicago."

Swann's first letter was from Chicago, too. Megan worried her lower lip for a few moments. "Iris—wasn't she from Illinois?"

"A *lot* of people are from Illinois," Bernie replied.

"Okay!" the director called. "Everybody take his position. Let's go for another take. And remember—*no sweat!*"

"I don't see how you do it," Megan remarked several hours later. She and Swann were standing at the rear entrance of the club, waiting for Kyle to bring the limousine around. She'd done a quick but careful survey of the area when they'd stepped outside. She hadn't noticed anything or anyone suspicious.

"Do what?" He stretched like a cat.

"The same song over and over again."

He laughed a little tiredly and reached for her hand. "No sweat, sugarplum," he answered, mimicking the video director perfectly. His expression grew thoughtful as his silver-gray eyes caressed her face. "I'm *so* glad you came today," he told her softly, reaching forward with his free hand to trace the curve of her lower lip. "It's good to have someone real to hang onto in all this make-believe."

Real. The word cut like a knife. Her feelings for Swann were real. But everything else . . .

"Megan?" Swann questioned, his dark brows coming together. "Is something wrong?"

"No," she responded quickly.

He took her by the shoulders. "Did Bernie or anybody else say anything to you?" he asked.

"I—what do you mean?" He was too perceptive, and she was fast losing the ability or the desire to go on deceiving him. But she knew she had to. As long as it was necessary to use subterfuge to protect him, that was what she would do.

"Something was said, wasn't it?" he asked. "I knew people would talk a little but I didn't—look, I'm sorry. People tend to be about as refined as crude oil when it comes to discussing my private life. I'm used to it by now. I barely hear it. But you—"

"It's all right, Swann," she told him. His concern touched her. So did his noticing her uneasiness on the set, despite everything else he must have had on his mind. "I—I just never thought of myself as a groupie before," she said lightly, trying to make a joke of it.

"A groupie?"

"Well, I know I don't exactly have the right look at this point," she said in the same teasing vein. She gestured deprecatingly at her cream denim jeans and cream, peach, and jade plaid shirt. Compared with the trendy get-ups she'd seen on the other women at the shoot, she definitely looked like Mary Poppins. "But I picked up a few fashion hints today."

"For example?" He circled her waist loosely with his arms.

"Oh—" She gazed at him, vaguely aware that Kyle had driven up to the curb and was getting out of the limousine. "Stiletto heels with sweatsuits. Sneakers with rhinestone-studded lingerie—"

Swann grinned, his teeth glinting against his tanned skin. "How about stiletto heels with rhinestone-studded lingerie?" he suggested with a mock leer.

Megan pretended to consider this. Kyle was marching around to open the right rear door of the car. "Hmm— I think that would be too much of one thing," she said.

Swann's eyes were as smoky as his voice. "Maybe. But even too much of that one thing is never enough."

With that, he tightened his embrace possessively, pulling her body against his and lowering his head to claim her mouth.

Afterward—a long, dazed time afterward—Megan wondered how long her younger brother had stood by the limousine's open door, pointedly clearing his throat, before she and Swann finally broke apart and got into the car.

"So, you had a good time with your grandmother, hmm?" Megan asked as she helped P.J. into bed that night.

"Yeah," he acknowledged. "Except for this wierd chicken with yucky sauce we had for dinner. I gave Buddy a little taste and he didn't like it, either." He wrinkled his nose. "Did you have a good time with Daddy?"

"Uh-huh," she replied briefly, bending to tuck in the sheets. For heaven's sake, Megan Louise, she scolded herself, it's a perfectly innocent question from a six-year-old!

"Did you miss me while I was at Grandma Sandra's?" P.J. wanted to know. There was a slight hesitation in his voice.

"Of course, I did," she assured him.

"Really?" he pressed.

"Really." Swann's son had been in an odd mood since he'd come back to the beach house. Megan wondered what the root of it was.

"I missed you, too," the little boy said. "And Daddy." He heaved a sigh. "I wish he didn't have to have a stupid practice tonight," he complained grumpily.

"Well, you know your father has to get ready for the Nightshade concert this weekend," she reminded him. In the midst of everything else, the band had a long-standing five-day engagement at the Universal Amphitheater in Universal City. All five of the performances had been sold out weeks before.

"Yeah, I guess," he conceded reluctantly. "Are you going?"

Megan hesitated. She had the feeling that P.J. was

working himself up to making some point with all these questions, but she wasn't certain what that point was. "Your father's invited me to go to the opening night," she replied, sitting on the edge of the bed. She and Patti had already discussed letting P.J. and Joey spend the night together under the supervision of one babysitter.

"You better look out for the pepperonis," he advised.

"Pepperonis?" she repeated, puzzled. She'd gotten to the point where she could usually figure out P.J.'s fractured versions of the big words he'd overheard; however, this time she drew a blank.

"You know, the guys who take pictures." He imitated the clicking of a camera. "The pepperonis. Grandma Sandra says they're pests."

"Oh—" She smiled. "The paparazzi."

"Yeah, them. Hey—if they bother you, you can throw them like you threw Mr. Bosley!"

"P.J.—"

"I told Grandma Sandra all about what you did."

"Did you?" She wasn't certain she wanted to learn what Alexandra's reaction to the story had been.

"Uh-huh. She was real interested. She asked me lots of stuff about you. She likes you."

She didn't quite know how to respond. "That—well, that's very nice to hear."

P.J. sighed again, his expression distinctly troubled.

Megan frowned. "P.J., is something the matter?"

He stared at her a moment and then glanced away, sticking out his lower lip. "I saw Daddy kiss you," he announced finally.

Megan shifted uncomfortably. She'd tried to be very discreet about her physical relationship with Swann around P.J. Obviously, she hadn't tried hard enough. "When was this?" she asked gently, stroking his forehead.

"A couple of days ago," he answered vaguely.

"Did it"—she searched for the right word—"did it bother you?"

"Not like when I saw the lady coming out of Daddy's room," he said, shaking his head. "But I mostly think kissing's pretty dumb." He looked at her. "I told Grandma Sandra."

"Oh." Megan flushed deeply, quickly reviewing Alexandra Collins's behavior when she and Swann had gone to her mansion to pick up P.J. It had been right after the video shoot. Had there been anything odd or different in her legendary, charming manner? Megan hadn't noticed anything at the time. She'd found Alexandra as warmly gracious as ever. And yet—

"And Grandma smiled," P.J. continued. "She went 'hmm-hm-m-m.' *Then* she told me I shouldn't spy on people." He blinked. "I wasn't spying, Megan. Honest and true. I just saw—"

She stroked his forehead again. "I know you weren't spying."

There was a break in the conversation. Megan kept quiet, sensing that the little boy wanted to say something more.

"Do you . . . do you like Daddy?" he asked at last.

"Yes, I do," she told him softly.

"More than you like me?" His eyes were wide.

"Oh, P.J.—sweetheart, it's not a matter of my liking him more than you. I like you both—very much. But in different ways."

No, a little voice told her, you *love* them both . . . in different ways. At least be honest about that!

P.J. swallowed. "Will you—will you stay with us forever, then?"

For a moment, Megan didn't trust herself to speak. "Forever is a long time," she said at last. She'd said over and over that time was what she needed. She had the sudden feeling that time was running out.

"I know, but—"

"And pretty soon you're going to be so grown up, you won't need a nanny."

"Well, yeah, I guess," he said after several moments of silence. "But—but even when I get big, we can still be friends. Friends for always. Just like in Daddy's song."

"Of course, we can be friends for always," she promised, and she hugged him.

P.J. seemed to hold on to her for a long, long time.

"Mmm—Swann?" Megan asked drowsily, roused from a deep, dreamless sleep by the feel of a lean, emphatically male body curving against hers. A pair of strong arms encircled her.

"I sure as hell hope you're not expecting anybody else," Swann answered, his distinctive voice husky with a mixture of exhaustion and amusement.

"How was rehearsal?"

"Not bad. Just don't ever let anybody tell you that a rock band can function as a democracy."

"Hmm?" Megan's impulse to pursue this point got lost as she felt Swann kissing the hollow behind her ear.

"What are you wearing?" he inquired.

"Wearing?" she repeated dreamily, snuggling back against him. She was still in that blissfully hazy state between sleep and wakefulness. The warmth of his body and the velvet richness of his voice cocooned her. But there was something . . . "I'm wearing . . . a nightgown."

He chuckled, his palms cupping her breasts through the soft cotton fabric. "I can feel that. I mean your perfume. It's . . . mmm . . . innocent but sexy."

"I'm not wearing perfume. It's just me."

"Ah, I should have guessed." He shifted her to make the fit of their bodies even more intimate. "Lord, do I need some sleep," he murmured through a yawn.

"How late—"

"Very." He yawned again. "I didn't mean to wake you. I just wanted to be close for a few hours. To hold you. Don't worry. I'll be out before P. J. gets up."

P.J.

Megan stiffened suddenly, her sleep-fogged brain clearing abruptly.

"Megan?" Swann questioned, responding to her change of mood almost instantly. "What's wrong?"

She turned in his arms, breathing in the clean male scent of him. "P.J.—Swann, P.J. saw you kiss me."

"Oh, that." Swann relaxed again, threading his fingers through her red-gold hair. "Yeah, I know."

"You know?" Although there was very little light in the room, she could just make out the shape of his features. She thought he was smiling. "Did P.J. tell you?"

"He told my mother and she told me. She and I had a talk while you were upstairs with him making sure he had all his stuff packed to come home."

"Swann—" She started to pull away from him, but he held her fast. His embrace was gentle but inescapable.

"It's all right, Megan," he said soothingly. "Remember what I told you Patti Guarino said when I arranged for P.J. to spend the night with Joey?"

"I—" It took her a moment to make the connection. "'It's about time.'" she quoted.

"Exactly. That was the general tenor of what my mother had to say during our little discussion."

"But—"

"She likes you, love."

She trembled at the endearment, hardly believing what she was hearing. "Your—your mother barely knows me!" she protested.

"My mother makes up her mind about people very quickly. She decided to marry my father after doing a five-minute reading for him for a part he didn't cast her in. And he claims *he* decided to marry *her* as soon as she walked into the audition. So it worked out fine."

"Still—"

"She's seen you with P.J. And with me." His voice was tender. It deepened as he added, "She knows you, Megan."

No. No, she doesn't, Megan thought with a pang. And you don't either, Swann . . . my love. Not really.

She took a deep breath. "Swann—"

"Shh." He hushed her with a kiss.

If she had known exactly what she wanted to say . . . and how she wanted to say it to him . . . Megan might have resisted. As it was, she allowed herself to be silenced.

Seeking . . . savoring. Giving . . . taking. Their lips met. Clung. Moved. Then clung again. The taste of him flooded her mouth and she caught the faintly minty flavor of his toothpaste. His tongue slid boldly through the slick barrier of her teeth, exploring the sweet recesses within with probing, provocative skill. She answered the erotic, evocative thrusts with darting little movements of her own tongue.

His hands roamed over her, burning and branding through the sheer fabric of her nightgown. Pleasure pinwheeled through her body. At that moment, there in the darkness, Colin Swann *did* know Megan Harper . . . utterly.

Megan reveled in his knowledge without shame, without uncertainty.

"I thought you needed rest," she whispered throatily, feeling him begin to tug the hem of her nightgown upward to her waist. His fingers drifted over her parted thighs, searching out the soft, downy delta that proclaimed her woman. "Swann—"

"I need you more."

CHAPTER EIGHT

"MEGAN? ARE YOU READY?"

"Just a second, Swann," she called, staring at her reflection anxiously. She made another tugging adjustment at the top of her dress. The fashionable assortment of gold bangles she wore on her left wrist clinked metalically.

How could Swann sound so calm? She knew he'd received yet another unsigned, ominously worded letter. Her father had read it to her over the phone the night before, and the language had made her sick. Even worse, the letter hadn't come through the mail. It had been left with the receptionist in the lobby of the recording studio where Nightshade was working. No one—including Kyle, who had been waiting out front with the limousine—had seen the person who had brought it. Or perhaps the person had been seen, but not noticed.

And, on top of everything else, Swann was supposed

to go out tonight and give a concert in front of more than five thousand people!

Frowning, she smoothed the malachite-green silk of her dress one last time. The garment was, without a doubt, the most deliberately provocative thing she had ever owned. It had a strapless, tightly wrapped bodice and a flirty, hip-skimming skirt that just brushed the tops of her knees. The rich fabric—shot here and there with traces of gold thread—complemented her fair complexion and fiery hair. The cut flattered her figure and emphasized her slender legs.

She'd spotted the dress in a store window two days before while shopping with Patti, P.J., and Joey. Had she been on her own, she probably would have resisted temptation. But Patti—after muting the boys' complaints with a promise of ice cream cones—had urged her to try it on. Once she'd slipped into the outrageously attractive, outrageously expensive garment, Megan's willpower had evaporated. Patti had clinched the sale by assuring her that the outfit was the perfect thing for tonight's concert.

After giving her mousse-styled hair a quick fluff, Megan coated her lashes with a final layer of black mascara and slicked another daub of coral lip gloss on her mouth. A swift *woosh* of Shalimar perfume and she was ready to go.

"Megan—" Swann's voice held a combination of amusement and impatience. "I'm sure the wait is going to be—"

Crossing the room, she opened the door to him.

"—worth it," he finished softly. His eyes flowed over her like molten metal, taking in every detail of her appearance from the sensual, artless disorder of her hair to the sleek elegance of her gold sandals.

"I'm sorry if I'm late," she apologized, having some trouble getting the words out. His expression seemed to have temporarily paralyzed her ability to breathe. Her pulse, on the other hand, was reacting as though she were mainlining Adrenalin.

"All of a sudden, I don't give a damn about what time it is," he responded, moving to within a few inches of her. Lifting his right hand, he trailed his index finger along the line of her collarbone with exquisite care. "You are very beautiful," he told her.

Blood, hot and honeyed, mantled Megan's shoulders, throat, and cheeks. "You—you don't think it's a bit much?" she asked. For a few moments, she allowed herself to forget about the secrets she was keeping . . . to forget about the nameless, faceless threat Swann was facing.

Swann gave her a slow, blisteringly sexy smile. "Will you take something off if I say yes?" His eyes ran over her again.

She moistened her lips. "Patti said this was the right sort of thing for the concert."

"Oh, it is."

"And she said the party afterward would be dressy—"

"True," he concurred, lifting her left hand to his lips. "But I don't think we'll be going to the party afterward."

"You . . . don't?" She caught her breath as he placed a searing kiss in the center of her palm. The contact was explicitly erotic. It triggered sparks that burned trails along her nervous system and then exploded into a liquefying cascade of sensation between her thighs.

"No," he confirmed, his mouth and tongue making incendiary promises against her flesh. "At least not *right* afterward."

"Where—where do you think we'll go first?" Lord, why hadn't she realized the palm was an erogenous zone?

Swann looked at her. "First, we'll go somewhere private."

Private probably was the last word in the world Megan would have picked to describe the wings of an arena stage five minutes before the start of a sold-out rock concert. Yet, as she stood in the wings of the Universal Amphitheater with Swann, waiting for his cue, private was the way she felt.

She also felt protected. In addition to several dozen uniformed security people, she'd already counted four operatives from Harper Security besides herself and Kyle. Lacking any concrete clues, her father had decided that there could be a link between the concert and the line "when the music stops for good" which had appeared in several of the letters. Simon Harper had reacted accordingly and taken special precautions.

Swann clasped her hands. "Your fingers are like ice!"

"I guess I'm nervous," she said. "Aren't—aren't *you?*"

He shook his head. Dressed in his signature black, with the trademark silver earring glinting against his night-dark hair, Swann was radiating an edgy, barely contained energy. It was as though some finely tuned engine were being revved up inside him. "I'm just itchy to get on."

"How long—?"

"A couple of minutes. Time to start a lot of things, but not enough to finish them." He was looking at her mouth when he answered. Megan's lips, which had been kissed clean of their coral gloss during the ride from Malibu, parted slightly.

"I'll be here when you come back," she promised.

"I'd find you if you weren't."

She was aware of the beginnings of a rumbling surge of applause. "Swann—" She wanted to say so many things in that instant. Good luck. Be careful. I love you.

He pulled her against him and kissed her, his mouth hot and hard and hungry. "You don't get any easier to leave, Megan," he told her. And then he was on.

The anticipatory applause swelled into ecstatic screams as he stepped on stage. The power of the response rolled

over the footlights with Richter-scale force. Standing
where she was, still trembling from his kiss, Megan could
feel the energy, the electricity, of it.

Swann seemed to accept it, absorb it, incite it. "Come
to watch us play?" Swann asked into the microphone,
his voice insinuating. The audience howled back an affirmative. His teeth gleamed white against his bronzed
skin. "Well," he drawled, "we wouldn't want to disap-
point any of you."

> I've been here before, babe:
> I said I'd be back.
> Look out. Trouble's coming.
> You know me, for sure, babe:
> Pulse is pounding. Feel the fever.
> Hear my heartbeat drumming—

Nightshade's first set sizzled. It was hard-driving, bad-
boy rock from start to finish, shorn of the studied, sophisticated musical complexities the band had a reputation for delivering in the recording studio. It was as clean
and as sharp as a razor blade—edged and more than a
little dangerous. Despite Megan's knowing the whole
thing had been choreographed and calculated—that each
riff had been rehearsed, each lighting change laid down
in a computer program—she was enthralled by the aura
of explosive spontaneity the band created.

The audience shrieked its approval as Boomer Jankowski committed something close to criminal assault
on his drum set. Coney Guarino, a man who was capable
of playing Mozart with crystalline precision, pounded
and punished his keyboard. Rick Nichols laid down a
wicked rhythm line that anchored all of them to the most
basic level.

Swann matched them, wildness for wildness. His style
was primitive and pagan and utterly passionate. Neither

he nor the audience needed a chance to warm to the other. They met head-on, eyes open, and going well over the speed limit.

Swann had done over thirty minutes of hard labor before he came off the stage for the first time. His eyes glittered. His nostrils flared as he sucked in deep, shuddering gulps of air. He stripped off his sweat-sodden shirt, mopped his perspiration-sheened torso with a towel, and donned another black top in what seemed to be a single, fluid motion. Someone handed him a glass of something clear and cold. He knocked it back in one swallow, reaching for his guitar even as he was returning the glass.

He said nothing to Megan, even though every fiber of her body told her he was aware of her. But there was a split second when he glanced her way, his gaze reaching out to her as though she were some infinitely precious talisman.

Then he was back out in the spotlight again.

This time, the songs were slower, more intensely wrought. If the first set had been hammered into heavy metal, this one was etched into glass with acid. The stage lighting transformed Swann into a compelling study in shadows and highlights as he sang of intimate angers, unspoken promises, and seductive strangers.

The music and the words were very much his own, filtered through his experiences, distilled through his artistry. But what made his performance of them so compelling was the way he held himself aloof from the emotions he invoked. He stood still as he sang, his austerely carved features closed off, his body language posting a No Trespassing sign. He didn't try to reach the audience. He didn't need to. They reached for him.

Megan ached for him in her heart, her mind . . . her body. She wanted to reach for him, too. She wanted to reach for him and hold him for the rest of her life.

The third set of songs was a slick combination of

Nightshade classics and new numbers. The audience was up and dancing in their seats by the time the band launched into the introduction to the second tune.

Tearing her eyes from what she was watching for just a moment, Megan glanced around. Everything backstage seemed to be as it should be. She got a brief nod and a swift thumbs-up sign from one of the Harper Security staffers as her gaze slid over him. She got a jealous but knowing look from a pert blonde she recognized from the video shoot and received a fast, friendly smile from Patti Guarino.

Kyle was standing about ten yards away, flirting with Bernie McGillis's curvy secretary. While he obviously had the young woman's full and enthusiastic attention, Megan could tell by the tension in his posture that he wasn't allowing himself to be genuinely distracted. Kyle was still on the job.

From him, Megan got a questioning stare that held what was getting to be a very familiar tinge of fraternal disapproval.

Out on the stage, the band broke loose, kicking into overdrive. They bounced solo licks and challenges back and forth as if they were basketballs. No one ever failed to catch what came to him.

"Hey!" Swann finally said, combing his fingers through his hair at the end of the band's third encore. His voice was rough and his breathing audibly harsh. "Don't you guys have anywhere to go?"

"No!" the audience roared back.

Swann laughed. He'd completely unbuttoned his shirt about twenty minutes before. Now he used the corner of the front of it to fan himself. Rick was fiddling with his guitar. Boomer was chugging down a bucket-size cup of something. Coney was watching Swann expectantly.

"Well, tough luck," Swann declared, "because I do."

The audience erupted into a cacophony of wolf whistles and suggestive but friendly shouts.

Swann laughed again, glancing toward one wing. Megan didn't think he could see her through the glare of the spotlight. Yet, his silver-gray gaze arrowed to her without hesitation, piercing her heart as though it had a target inscribed on it.

"One last song," Swann said. "I've got somebody waiting. And as much as I like all of you—to say nothing of Coney, Rick, and Boomer—I'd rather be with her."

And then he sang that one last song.

> Lady, lady, lover bright,
> Took a blind man, gave him sight;
> Took his hand, made him feel;
> Touched his heart, made him real.
> Lover, lover, lady light,
> You're the candle. No more night...

Afterward, Megan tried to recall exactly how she and Swann got to his private dressing room. She could remember being moved beyond words, moved close to tears, by the time he walked off the stage and into her wide-flung arms. And she could remember him sweeping her up and carrying her through the jostling, jabbering, backstage crowd.

But the details of what happened between the time Swann sang the last note of his song and the moment she realized they were locked in his dressing room, alone, remained vague. Considering some of the accounts she heard later, she eventually decided that probably was just as well. And, even though she never recovered all her gold bangles, she got her gold sandals back, thanks to the intervention of Bernie McGillis.

Memory—vivid and voluptuous—began when Swann turned away from the door he had slammed shut and locked after placing her on her feet. His expression was naked as he faced her; his strong, sensual features were taut with emotion. All he said was her name. He didn't really need to say that. Megan saw who she was . . . and what she meant to him . . . in his brilliant silver eyes.

They clung to each other first, buffeted by the strongest impulses known to man or woman. It didn't matter that there was a crowd of people on the other side of the door. The other side of the door didn't exist.

Megan reached up, burrowing her fingers through Swann's dark, damp tangle of hair and pulling his head down as she tilted hers back in eloquent offering. The molten desire she saw blazing in her lover's eyes set fire to her soul. It made her weak with wanting—too weak to look directly into the inferno of his gaze for more than a few moments. Her eyelids fluttered shut as his mouth slanted voraciously across hers, sealing it in a fierce, feverish kiss.

One of his arms claimed the slim circle of her waist, hauling her close, chaining her flat against him. She could feel the proud thrust of his arousal. She moved against him bonelessly, brazenly.

He shifted their positions in one fluid movement, pressing her back until she was sandwiched between the hardness of the wall and that of his body. The passion he poured into her, onto her, over her, seemed to have been pent up inside him for days . . . weeks . . . years . . .

His free hand inched slowly, sweetly, up her ribs until his fingers found the untrammeled undercurve of her breast. He toyed with the quivering flesh, his touch as delicate as his kiss was devouring.

He wooed her skillfully through the silk of her dress, making her twist and turn against him. He drank in her throaty cries of pleasure as though they were the sweetest wine he'd ever been offered.

Megan had his shirt partially off, running her fingers greedily through his chest hair, seeking out the sensitive buds of his male nipples, feeling him shudder in response. She stroked her palms around to his back, letting her hands stray like wanton explorers. His well-toned muscles rippled and released. The scent of his on-stage exertions clung to him and she inhaled it deeply, the masculine muskiness hazing her brain like an exotic incense.

The zipper of her dress was cunningly concealed in the left side seam of the bodice. Swann located it without fumbling and pulled it down in a swift, smooth motion. The garment fell away from her breasts, puddling briefly about her waist. Then it surrendered to gravity, sliding over her hips and falling to the floor in a whispering ripple of silk.

"Oh, Megan—" Swann sighed.

She was naked except for a pair of sheer satin briefs, a lacy garter belt, and pale, sheer stockings. If there were a moment to be shy with Swann, this was it. But Megan wasn't shy. She'd dressed herself in this lingerie with just such a moment in mind.

"Megan," he continued hoarsely, "I wish you could see yourself through my eyes . . . to know how beautiful . . . how perfect—"

"No—" She denied it with a shake of her head. "Not perfect, Swann."

"Yes, love."

He prepared her naked, aching breasts with his teeth and tongue, priming them for a pleasure so intense it was nearly pain. He sucked the beckoning, burgeoning crests into his mouth . . . first one, then the other . . . making her whimper and writhe.

Megan made a sound of protest when he abandoned her breasts. She made a second as he dropped to his knees in front of her.

"Swann—"

It was hard to speak, breathe, or think when his strong musician's hands played over her derrière and pulled her to him. It was harder still when she felt the press of his mouth against the fragile silk that covered the red-gold triangle at the juncture of her thighs. Swann had loved her this way before, lavishing her with the gentlest and most generous of caresses. And he had guided her tenderly, tutoring her with his groans of undisguised satisfaction, when she had sought to match his unselfishness.

"Swann—*no*—" She sobbed, clasping at his panther-black hair.

He stopped, still cupping her bottom.

She swayed, staring down at him. "I want *you*..." she said. "All of you... I want us *together*—"

He was on his feet a heartbeat later, moving with the jungle-cat grace she would always see as uniquely his.

"Together," he promised.

Swiftly they rid each other of what few clothes they still had on, their path to the large, luxuriously upholstered sofa in the corner of the dressing room punctuated by carelessly discarded garments.

They tumbled down onto the sofa... together.

Swann's presence filled her mind. The taste of him filled her mouth.. And the maleness of him filled her hand as she closed her fingers about him.

They sought completion... together.

Shaking like a flower petal in a wind storm, Megan opened herself to him. Swann clasped her hard, controlling the rhythm for a few seconds. He soothed her desperate haste with kisses and caresses, bringing them into perfect attunement.

"Swann, *please*—" She was urgent, aching... empty without him.

"Yes, love, yes. Now."

And they found what they were seeking... together.

At the height of their quest, with the prize within both their grasps, they said the same three words... together.

"*I... love... you.*"

"Did you mean—" Megan began but then stopped. She turned her face into Swann's shoulder.

He wouldn't let her avoid the inquiry or the answer.

Weaving his fingers through her thoroughly tousled hair, he forced her to look at him. "Yes, I *mean* it," he told her steadily. "I love you, Megan."

She closed her eyes for a moment, wondering how she could feel utterly fulfilled and completely frightened at the same time.

"Did you mean it?" he asked.

She opened her eyes. "Oh, yes," she told him fervently. "Oh, yes, I love you, Swann."

He touched her cheek. His eyes were intent on her face. She had the feeling he was searching for something.

The truth. What was real.

"Swann—" She had to tell him. She had to tell him *now*. "I have to talk—"

There was a sharp rap on the door, and the other side of the locked dressing room door suddenly popped back into existence.

"I know," he said, a flash of frustration appearing in his expression. *"We* have to talk."

"Yes, Swann—"

Knock! Knock!

"In a minute!" Swann called savagely. He took Megan's hands and raised them to his mouth, brushing his lips along her knuckles. "We can't do it now. We'll talk tomorrow morning. We have a whole hell of a lot to say to each other."

"Minute?" Bernie McGillis's voice grated through the door. "Dammit, Swann, it's been nearly an *hour!*"

"Your public calls," Megan observed wryly. "Tomorrow morning, then."

He nodded. "Before we go pick up P.J." The smile he gave her held passion—and a promise. *"Together."*

Given a choice, Megan wouldn't have gone to the post-concert party at all, and, neither, she suspected, would have Swann. But they didn't really have a choice. Swann had to go because he was the star and the star had responsibilities. And she had to go because...

Because she wanted to be with him? Yes, that was part of it. She couldn't bear the idea of being separated from him, not this night, not after what had happened between them. But that desire to stay close, to draw near, wasn't all of it.

Megan Louise Harper wasn't a star. She'd never aspired to be. She was what she was. She, too, had responsibilities.

Being in love with Colin Swann didn't diminish her identity or what she had to do. It changed things, true. And it made them more complicated. But it didn't diminish her in any way. If anything, it freed her to flourish.

At least... that was what she hoped.

Tomorrow, she would explain everything to Swann. She would find a way to make him understand how she had come into his life and why she wanted to remain a part of it. Swann had given her the time. She—finally—would give him the truth. All of it. And surely, if he'd meant the words he'd said, the words he'd written and sung, it would be all right between them.

The hardest part of going to the party—aside from having to face Kyle and a horde of photographers getting in and out of the limo—was walking into the private club where it was being held. Megan wasn't an insecure woman, and she was feminine enough to enjoy making a grand entrance now and again, but stopping a hundred conversations cold simply by stepping through a doorway was almost more than she could handle.

It *would* have been more than she could handle if Swann hadn't nonchalantly slipped his arm around her waist, painted the motionless room with a quicksilver stare, and drawled, "Well, Megan, my love, it appears we are a trifle tardy to this little soirée."

With that, a hundred new conversations erupted out of a silence that had been so profound that Megan could have sworn she'd heard an olive plop into a martini.

She spent most of the night within the circle of Swann's arm. That meant that she stayed center stage and in the spotlight. Had she been on her own, she would have preferred the wings, the shadows. But as long as she was with him . . .

Swann showed her off with unmistakable pride even as he sheltered her with almost primitive possessiveness. In countless ways—some as subtle as a smile, some as savage as a rattlesnake glare at a man whose tongue had been loosened by liquor—he made it clear that Megan Harper was his . . . and that he was hers.

There was a brief conversation with Bernie McGillis, who was pleasant but clearly not entirely pleased by how *extremely* close she had gotten to his client. There was a funny chat with Boomer Jankowski, who had belatedly recognized her as the woman he'd plied with Chloroform Cocktails. Rick Nichols materialized with an unfamiliar companion—dubbed Georgia Peach although her name was Tammi and she was from Texas. And Coney and Patti carried on as though Megan and Swann had been an item for years.

Megan was aware of a lot of things—legal and otherwise—being smoked, sniffed, sipped, and snacked on by the people circulating around her. She kept her glass filled with ginger ale. Swann, she noticed, had one Scotch and then drank nothing but mineral water.

He invited her into his world and she went willingly, wonderingly, after that one horrible hesitation in the doorway. But even while Swann was sharing this part of his life with her, she knew he wanted to keep her separate . . . special.

"So," he murmured into her hair about two hours after their arrival, "are you beginning to develop a new sense of sympathy for the victims of the Spanish Inquisition?"

He was maneuvering her about the dance floor with languid skill. The band was playing a slow love ballad.

"You mean, all the questions?"

"Mmm. If I get one more leering inquiry about what I was getting into after Nightshade's last encore, I may break somebody's capped front teeth." Their bodies moved in unthinking unison.

"Well, we weren't exactly discreet," she reminded him.

"We locked the door. In this business, that qualifies as discreet."

"You know what I mean. After you sang that song—" She melted a little at the memory. The love in those lyrics made the unpleasantries of the party seem trivial. It seemed impossible that anything . . . anyone . . . could hurt either of them.

"You like the song?" he asked, holding her closer.

"It's beautiful," she told him with radiant sincerity.

"You're the one who's beautiful."

"What was it Patti said I had? Oh, yes. The rumpled, ravished look."

"Beautiful," he repeated.

"I just wish people wouldn't keep staring at me. I feel as though my slip is showing."

"If memory serves, love, you don't have a slip to show."

"True."

Swann pressed his lips against the side of her neck, tasting the soft skin. "It won't always be this bad," he told her.

"Actually," Megan admitted slowly, "it's turned out better than I expected. People—most of them—have been nice. Almost *too* nice." She laughed lightly. "I'm beginning to feel like the latest official mistress of Louis the Fourteenth or something. Being fawned over, having my favor—Swann?"

He pulled back slightly, his expression taut.

"I was only joking," she said.

"A lot of women like being fawned over," he observed in an odd tone. She wondered if he were referring to Iris

Ames—or any of the other women from his past.

Lifting her palm, she laid it against his cheek. "I'm not a lot of women."

"No." He pulled her back against him. "You're a lot of *woman.*"

They had to run the gauntlet of press people again when they left. Megan knew a few moments of fear, remembering the defaced amateur photographs that had accompanied the most recent letters. Could the person who had been sending those letters be hiding in the jostling, shouting crowd of journalists and gossip hounds? She flinched slightly as a flash bulb went off in her face.

Swann's reaction was more mundane. He simply kept a tight grip on Megan's elbow and ignored everyone else as he muscled a path to their waiting limousine. He handed her into the car and slipped in beside her. Kyle slammed the door shut a lot harder than was necessary.

Megan settled back, letting herself relax again.

"Damn paparazzi," Swann muttered, slipping an arm around her bare shoulders.

She leaned her head against him. "Pepperonis," she repeated, sighing.

"What?"

"P.J. calls them pepperonis," she explained with a small laugh. "He told me to watch out for them."

It was a pity someone hadn't told her to watch out for Lewis Bosley.

CHAPTER NINE

SHE HAD ABSOLUTELY no warning.

One moment, she was fast asleep, sprawled in boneless, blissful abandon in her lover's bed. The next moment, she was fully awake, with the sheets she had wrapped around her body being ripped away by a man whose anger made him a total stranger.

"Swann—?" she faltered in disbelief, her head spinning at the abrupt transition. She struggled to sit up. Her mouth was cottony-dry, her eyes wide. She shielded herself from him instinctively, crossing shaking arms in front of her naked breasts.

"Get up. Get dressed. Get out," he repeated, spitting the words at her contemptuously. He was towering over her like some vengeful creature from a nightmare. He was trembling with rage. Beneath his tan, he was very pale. His eyes were like dry ice—frigid but capable of burning to the bone. There were whitened indentations at both corners of his mouth.

"Swann, what—?"

"I had a call from Lewis Bosley this morning."

"Bosley?"

"That's right. It seems he got curious about the broad who got the best of him in McDonald's parking lot. So, once he got back to his feet, he did some digging. And guess what he found? That the woman I hired to take care of my son—the woman who's been sharing my house and my bed—is really Megan Harper of Harper Security, Incorporated!"

"Swann—"

He swore. "Get up and get dressed *now,* Megan. Or I swear to God I'll toss you out just the way you are."

Turning on his heel, he stalked out of the room.

Megan stared after him, trembling violently. "Oh, Lord," she moaned despairingly. "Oh, dear Lord, no!"

It was tomorrow morning and Colin Swann knew the truth.

Megan got out of the big bed, looking around distractedly. Get dressed. She had to do that.

She stumbled out of Swann's room and back to her own where she threw on a denim skirt, pulled on a hastily grabbed top, and stuffed her feet into a pair of shoes. She caught a glimpse of herself in a mirror as she headed for the door. Her face was sickly white, her features pinched.

She had to make him understand. *She had to!* She loved him. And he'd said he loved her. Somehow, some way, she had to put things right again.

He was standing by the glass doors in the living room when she came down the stairs at a reckless pace. The sunlight streaming in from outside was not kind to him. It revealed with uncompromising harshness the bitter depths of his disillusionment.

"Swann—"

"Damn you." He put the two words up like a wall, halting her in her tracks, shutting her out and off.

"No." She shook her head. "You don't understand."

"Oh, yes, I do."

It was like hearing a death knell, but she couldn't—wouldn't!—accept it. "You don't!" she persisted, flinging her hands wide. "You have to let me explain what—"

"Bernie McGillis has already explained. He went behind my back and hired some bodyguards. You were the ace in the hole. The one on the inside. You were supposed to get close and stay close." He pronounced the word *close* as though it were the vilest epithet imaginable.

"No, please—"

"Well, congratulations," he went on inexorably, cutting her off without raising his voice. The venom in his tone was murderous. "You certainly got close."

"It wasn't supposed to happen this way!" she cried.

"What? You mean I wasn't supposed to find out?"

"I was going to tell you!"

"When?"

"This morning!" She clenched her fists, willing him to understand . . . at least a little. "I tried to tell you last night, dammit! I did. *I did!* In the dressing room after we—"

"I don't want to hear about that!" For a moment, the air around them vibrated with the violence of his muted shout. Megan stared at him, shocked by his explosive loss of control.

"Swann—" she said again, reaching out.

He warned her off with his eyes. When he spoke, his voice was even once again.

"You lied to me," he said. It wasn't so much an accusation as a condemnation. She'd been tried and found guilty. This was her execution. "You lied to me about who you are and what you are."

She licked her lips. "All right, yes—"

" '*All right, yes?*' " he mocked viciously.

"It was my job!" she defended herself. "In the beginning, it was my *job*, Swann. Can't you see that? *Won't* you see that? For goodness' sake, I tried not to get involved with you. I told you, over and over and over, that it—*we*—were a mistake. Don't you remember?"

"You lied."

"Yes, I lied!" she screamed, and then pressed quaking fingers to her lips. She kept them there for a few awful seconds, afraid of what she might scream next. Finally, regaining her control, she took them away. "Dammit, Swann, somebody's been threatening you—following you! Somebody may want to *kill* you! If you hadn't been so dammed stubborn about not wanting—"

"This is my fault? Your lying is *my* fault?"

"No, of course not! It—I—" What could she say? Nothing. Everything. The only thing that mattered. "I love you, Swann."

"If you do, that's your problem."

She felt as though he'd struck her, but she refused to give up. "You said you love me."

"That's mine."

She opened her mouth to speak again but was silenced by the chime of the doorbell. The sound of it—everyday, ordinary—was shocking. "What—?"

The smile that curved Swann's lips was unpleasant. "I'd say that's probably your brother."

"My—my brother?" Oh, Lord, he *did* know everything!

He nodded. "Your brother, Kyle. Remember? The actor? The one who blends in with the background?" Megan made a small sound of protest as he named her untruths. "Bernie explained all about him, too."

"But what—"

"I thought there was something . . . fitting . . . about having him drive you away."

"What if I tell you I won't be driven away?" she challenged.

Swann said nothing. He just looked at her.

The doorbell chimed again.

And still Swann said nothing.

Megan's brief moment of bravado shattered. "What about P.J.?" she asked desperately.

The expression in his eyes made her flinch. "You lied to him, too, didn't you? You *used* him."

There was nothing she could say to that. Not now. Not when Swann had so obviously put up every barrier he could devise to use against her.

"My . . . my things?"

"I'll have them packed and sent to you." His tone implied the sooner her belongings were out of his house, the better. "I'm sure Bernie has your address."

"Swann—" She took her courage and caring in both hands. "If I—what are you going to tell P.J.?"

For a second, she thought she might have broken through his defenses. Then all hope died.

"I don't know. Maybe the truth." He didn't explain what that truth was. "Get out, Megan."

She did.

The limousine was halfway back to Los Angeles before Kyle spoke. She was sitting in the front seat next to him, staring at her fingers.

"Megan, look—" he began to say, his eyes on the road, his handsome young features grim.

"Kyle, please, don't give me a lecture," she begged in a choked voice. "I know I blew it." She had. She'd blown it all—professionally as well as personally. "I— no lecture. Not now."

He let a few seconds go by. "I wasn't going to give you a lecture," he said.

She glanced at him. She hadn't forgotten the looks she'd gotten from him. "Not even a fraternal I-told-you-so?" she asked with a trace of gallows humor.

"Nope. Not even that," he confirmed, the barest wisp of a smile passing over his mouth. "At least, not now. Besides, I never really *told* you anything about this—

him—uh, about what you were getting into."

"But you have very expressive eyes, Kyle," she informed him. She swallowed, telling herself that a little brother-sister bickering was better than breaking down and weeping.

Kyle didn't pretend he didn't know what she meant. "Yeah well, I was your brother before I was a chauffeur."

"Swann thought you had a thing for me," she recalled.

"What?"

"He noticed you staring at me. When he mentioned it, I said I'd only seen you staring at him."

"Oh, great."

"I had to say something, Kyle. I suggested that maybe he was the one you had a thing—"

"Thanks, Megan," he said. "Okay. okay. So I haven't exactly been Mr. Cool on this case. I admit it. But, as I said, I'm your brother." He paused, changing lanes. "Look, where do you want to go?"

"Go?" she repeated blankly. She hadn't even considered that. The one place she *wanted* to go—back to the beach house to try to reason with Swann—plainly wasn't a feasible suggestion. "I don't—to my apartment, I guess. Unless—" She felt a little sick. "I suppose I'd better go to the office. I have to explain. To file a report—"

"Dad has a pretty good idea of what went down," Kyle declared flatly.

"Did Swann—?"

"No. McGillis talked to him. Swann called *me* to pick you up. Geez, the guy has a tongue like a buzz saw!"

She gave a mirthless laugh. "I know. I walked into it."

"Right." Kyle switched lanes again. "Do you want to go to your apartment?"

"I—" She massaged her temples. She felt awful.

"Dad told me to tell you that you have the day off. He seems to think you might need it."

She was going to need more than a single day off if she couldn't find a way to put things back together with

Swann. Lord, she loved him so much.

"Hey, Meg?" Kyle prompted gently.

She sniffed. She wasn't going to cry in front of her younger brother. "Take me to my apartment."

She cried there. Alone.

"Well, I guess there's no real need to ask how you are," Patti Guarino said without preamble as she dropped into the seat next to Megan.

"No, I don't suppose there is," Megan acknowledged, fiddling with a cup of lemonade. It was forty-eight hours after her departure from Swann's beach house. She and Patti were at Cassell's Patio Hamburgers in the Wilshire district. It wasn't much of a place in terms of decor— yellow Formica tables with bridge chairs and semishiny linoleum floors, that sort of thing. But it did, in the opinion of many Angelenos, serve the best hamburgers in town. Unfortunately, Megan couldn't eat.

Patti didn't seem to have any such problem. She was regarding her juicy, all prime USDA-grade beef hamburger with something close to lust.

"To tell you the truth, Megan," she remarked, "the sunglasses wouldn't be such a dead giveaway if it weren't so overcast."

Megan nodded wearily. "I—I suppose you know everything."

"Well, the main witness for the prosecution—Swann— was a little less than cooperative, but I think I've pieced together most of what happened. I also had a little chat with Bernie. He's cringing in the corner of his office at the moment."

"Cringing—"

"Mmm." Patti bit into her burger, chewed, and swallowed. "He's gotten over being afraid Swann might break his neck with a karate chop. Now he's afraid he's going to break his contract."

"Oh, no!"

"Not to worry. When Bernie McGillis signs somebody, he stays signed."

Megan stared at the table. The sunglasses probably were a pretty pitiful ploy, but her eyes were still too red and puffy to be seen in public. "I'm surprised you asked me to have lunch with you if you know what happened."

"I think ordered you to have lunch with me is a more accurate version. And as for what happened—you were hired to do a job, right? So you did it. You didn't plan to fall in love with Swann. You didn't plan to have him fall in love with you."

Megan looked up. "I lied to him." She'd been lied to. She knew the hurt . . . the sense of betrayal.

"There are lies and there are lies, for heaven's sake."

"Not to Swann. I think—he must hate me now."

"Oh, yes. I'm sure. That's why he told Boomer he'd deck him if he mentioned your name any time in the next century."

"He what?"

"Don't worry. Swann settled for smashing his guitar on-stage. The audience at the Amphitheater went crazy. Of course, he nearly electrocuted himself—"

"Oh, Lord, is he all right?" Megan gripped the table, feeling herself grow pale. If anything happened to Swann—

Patti reached over and patted her fingers. "He's in about the same shape you are."

"Patti—"

"Look, sweetie, if it's any consolation, the guys in the band are all on your side. Especially about this bodyguard-threatening letter business. That was a real shock —those letters. I could kill Swann for acting like such a—" Patti broke off abruptly as Megan went completely white. "Oh, Megan, I'm sorry. What a stupid way to put it—"

"I'm so worried about him," Megan confessed painfully. "Not knowing who or when or *why*—" She shuddered. She'd spent much of the previous day going over and over the agency's file on Swann, trying desperately to make some sense out of the letters. She'd come up with nothing. She still didn't know who the "her" in the letters was . . . or what the number five signified. The only thing she was certain of was that, whether he admitted it or not, Swann's hang-up about security—and her own professional failure—made the man she loved vulnerable to harm.

"Look, those letters may not be anything more than words," Patti said. "Coney used to get postcards from some nut in New Jersey who accused him of being an advance scout for the planet Zoltran Three. The guy actually showed up at a concert. Except for the fact that he'd shaved his head and wrapped it in aluminum foil, he was . . . well, he smelled to high heaven, but he turned out to be perfectly harmless."

Megan shook her head. "I don't think this is the same."

"Okay, okay. But now that it's out in the open, Swann's got a lot of people looking out for him—whether he likes it or not." Patti took a drink of her lemonade.

"He won't like it," Megan returned flatly. Then she burst out, "Oh, God, Patti. He was so angry with me. I'd never seen him like that."

"Hardly anybody's ever seen him like that," Coney's wife stated. "Don't you realize what that means? Swann's angry because he's hurt and he's hurt because he loves you and you weren't honest. You reached him, Megan. You got inside all those damned defenses of his. And Lord knows, he's got enough of them. Not without good reason. That whole mess when he was growing up would have screwed anybody up. And then there was Iris— you want to talk about *lies*? But you got through to him. Despite everything. And no matter what he thinks—what you think—you didn't do it by being dishonest. Not in any way it counts."

Megan remained silent.

Patti leaned forward, her expression serious, her tone persuasive. "Swann never, ever lost his temper about Iris. Yes, he got angry with her, but that was only when P.J. was involved. Swann never loved Iris. There wasn't much—if anything—there to love. But he loves P.J. And he loves you!"

"And I love him," Megan murmured after a few seconds.

The next night, Swann's mother called her at home.

"Megan? It's Alexandra Collins."

Megan was sitting on the sofa in the small living room of her apartment. She'd been contemplating the two suitcases and a cardboard box Swann had sent over from the beach house. There hadn't been a note. Just a delivery form to sign. She hadn't been able to bring herself to unpack.

"Oh—" Her heart had leaped for one mad instant when the phone rang. Now it plunged. "Lady Swann."

"Alexandra. Please. I'd like you to call me Alexandra. And I'd like to go on calling you Megan, if you don't mind. I've gotten used to thinking of you that way."

"No, I don't mind," Megan told her quietly.

"Megan, I feel absolutely dreadful about what's happened."

Megan didn't ask what the older woman knew or how she knew it. "It's not your fault."

"I'm afraid it is, in a way. Aside from the fact that I'm the one whose maternal instincts overreacted so badly when my son was young—do you know about that?"

"I understand how Colin developed his allergy to bodyguards, yes. But I also understand why you did what you did."

"I was frightened. Unfortunately, I let my fears get out of hand. And, looking back, I realize I turned what should have been the freedom of childhood into something of a prison. With the best of intentions, yes. Still—" Alexandra Collins sighed. "Megan, I also knew all about your real reasons for taking the job as P.J.'s nanny."

"You—you did?" Megan once again remembered the conspiratorial smile the actress had given her the first day they'd met. She also recalled her odd behavior the day she'd delivered the puppy for P.J.

"Yes. Bernie McGillis enlisted my help."

"He never said—"

"No, he wouldn't. He's a very devious man. Although, in this instance, his motives were good. In any case, I was prepared to be in your corner, so to speak, the day you came to meet P.J. Of course, when you walked out to the terrace, I suspected you could turn out to be something very special. And when I saw the way my son behaved toward you—"

"I didn't behave much better."

"My dear, one day you must let me tell you the story of how my husband and I met."

"I already know a little about it."

"Ah." It was a very knowing sound. "Colin, no doubt."

"Yes," Megan confirmed. "But Lady—Alexandra—"

"Megan, this is more than a sympathy call," the older woman cut in. "I need your help. With P.J."

"P.J.?" Megan clutched the phone. She'd been very worried about the little boy. All Patti had been able to tell her the day before was that he was living with his glamorous grandmother again. She'd wanted to write, call, *something*, but not until she knew where things stood. "Is he all right?"

"He's upset and confused. Colin hasn't been very direct with him. P.J. came to live with me for a while."

"I—"

"I was wondering if you'd talk to him for a few minutes."

"But his father—"

"Megan, my concern is my six-year-old grandson. The fact that my thirty-five-year-old son is behaving like a—a—*whatever* it is he's behaving like is something I'll contend with later. Now, please—"

"Put P.J. on."

There was a pause. Then a small voice said, "Megan?" Her eyes pricked. "Hi, P.J."

"Daddy said you had to go away."

"I—"

"Did I do something bad?"

"Oh, no, P.J. Of course not!"

"I'll never do it again!" he burst out, ignoring her denial. "I'll be good, I promise. Forever and ever. Just come back, Megan." His voice started to go up.

"Sweetheart, please—you didn't do anything bad."

"You said you were going to stay! You said you *liked* me. You said we could be friends for always. Really—"

"P.J., I do like you—more than any little boy in the whole world." It was true. Without realizing it, she'd come to think of Peter Jordan Swann as almost her own. "We can be friends—"

"Did *Daddy* do something bad to you?" he asked with the sudden, disastrously acute intuition of a child.

Megan bit the inside of her lip. No matter what else happened, no matter how this situation between herself and Swann turned out, she couldn't let the relationship between father and son be damaged. She cared far too much for both of them.

"Megan?" There was a wobble in P.J.'s voice.

"No. Your father didn't do anything bad to me." She willed herself not to cry. "He and I are still friends."

"Then why did you go away?"

"I had to. It's—I—it's a grown-up thing. You . . . it's something you'll understand when you get older."

"Daddy said that, too."

"Did he?"

"Yeah." There was a long silence. "Megan, will you come and see me?"

"P.J., I can't right now." She heard a sniff from the other end of the line. "Maybe in a few days," she temporized. "How's Buddy doing?"

The puppy ploy failed miserably as a diversionary tactic.

"I think he's sick. He misses you."

"I'm sure you'll take care of him. What about Godzilla?"

The gerbil gambit didn't work either. "He misses you, too."

"Well..." She took a steadying breath. "Will you let me talk to your grandmother again?"

"O–kay." The word came dragging out.

"Megan?" Alexandra Collins said a second later. "Something has to be done."

Megan sighed. "I know. I know. I just need to figure out what to do and how to do it."

"My dear, I might be able to—"

Megan saw what was coming and rejected it. "No," she cut in. "Alexandra, thank you, but *no*. I have to—no."

"I see." There was a pause. "Will you come to visit P.J.?"

Megan felt a prickle of apprehension. She liked Alexandra Collins; she genuinely did. But she had the feeling the older woman could more than match Bernie McGillis when it came to deviousness. That deviousness might serve in some situations. Not this one. There had been enough deception between her and Swann.

"I'll come, Alexandra," Megan replied slowly, "if you'll give me your word that P.J. is the only person I'll see."

The actress cleared her throat very delicately. "Megan, my dear, if I didn't realize how upset you are, I'd be hurt—"

"I need your word."

There was a brief silence. "I only want what's best for my son. And I happen to believe that's you."

Megan didn't say anything.

Alexandra clicked her tongue. "You have my word."

"Aren't you ever going home?" Kyle demanded late the next night as he ambled into Megan's office and perched himself on the edge of her desk.

"Aren't you?" she countered, reaching for a bottle of correction fluid. She suspected her younger brother was sticking around at the agency out of concern for her.

Kyle shrugged vaguely, fingering through the pages she had been typing. "Is this the report on Swann?"

Megan nodded, whiting out a misspelling. "It's been four days. I decided I'd better get everything down. Dad's been terrific, but I know his patience isn't going to last forever."

Kyle grunted his agreement. "Look—uh—Megan . . . when you say *everything*, just how much—uh—territory does that include?"

Something about the tone of this stumbling question made her look up sharply. "Why do you ask?"

"I—" He shifted uncomfortably. "I don't think you—uh—need to put in the stuff about the pool."

She felt her cheeks flame. For one crazy second, she wondered if Harper Security's surveillance of Swann's home had been even more elaborate than she'd known. "What makes you think there should be any stuff about the pool to include?"

Her brother grimaced. "You know how Eddie Ramirez was working with the pool service? Well . . . he found a pair of your panties in the pool filter."

"What?" A note or two higher and her voice would have shattered glass.

"It was a day or so after you decked Bosley. A bunch of us in the agency had been kidding around about Swann's reputation with women. I guess I said something about my getting more action than he did. You know, that I hadn't seen any evidence—"

"So Eddie brought you some evidence," she concluded with a groan. "But how did you know they were mine?"

"Steve recognized them as part of that nightgown set Joan bought you for your birthday."

"Oh." She shook her head. "No wonder you kept glaring—" She broke off as an awful thought hit her. "Does Dad—?"

"No. Oh, look, he knows there was something between you and Swann. But there's no need to give him the . . . you know."

"The graphic details?" She experienced a fleeting sense of amusement at Kyle's uncharacteristic awkwardness.

"Yeah."

There was a long silence. Megan rubbed the back of her neck. She hadn't been sleeping at all well.

"You're really hung up on him, aren't you?" Kyle asked with sudden gentleness, his good-looking face growing serious.

"I love him," she said simply. She clenched her fists. "And I'm so *worried* about him, Kyle."

"Yeah." Kyle's expression became distinctly troubled. "Meg . . . I wasn't going to tell you, but there was another letter."

"What?" She sat upright, eyes wide. "How do you—?"

"Sheila. McGillis's secretary. You know, the cute blonde. I—I know the agency's off the case, but I hate the idea of unfinished business. And, hell, I'm not stupid.

I've got a damned good idea of what it would do to you if anything happened to Swann."

"Kyle!"

"Anyway, I asked Sheila to keep her eyes and ears open. As sort of a personal favor."

Megan didn't need to ask why Sheila might be inclined to do her younger brother a personal favor. "What did the letter say?"

"Pretty much the same crap. Except for a line at the end: 'You'll meet me like you met her.'"

"You'll meet me like you..." she repeated slowly. There was something familiar about the words. But what? *what?* She juggled the clues, the hints, the possibilities.

"Megan?" Kyle asked suddenly, sounding genuinely alarmed.

"Oh, no," she whispered, turning to him. Her heart was pounding. *"Her.* It has to be Iris Ames. It *has* to be. Swann had met her backstage after a concert. *When the music stops for good.* And Kyle—" She stood up, shaking. "The number five on those photographs—this is Nightshade's *fifth* concert at the Amphitheater—"

"Let's go."

CHAPTER TEN

IT WAS A tribute to Kyle's defensive driving skills—and pure luck—that they reached the Universal Amphitheater in record time without being stopped for speeding. Nonetheless, Megan had the horrible feeling that they might be too late. The concert was already letting out as they arrived. People were streaming out of the brightly lighted hall, heading in scores of different directions.

"Try to go around to the stage entrance," Megan ordered her younger brother urgently. She glanced at the dashboard clock. Had something happened? Had the concert been cut short? The opening night performance had run nearly thirty minutes longer than this!

"This damned traffic," Kyle cursed, trying to maneuver through openings that didn't really exist. "I—look out, you idiot!" He punched the horn, thoroughly startling the dozen or so concertgoers who were unwisely trying to cross in front of him.

171

She had to do something. After a split second of consideration, she did it.

"Megan, what the—?" her brother exploded, making a grab for her.

She was out of the car, the door slammed shut behind her, before he had a chance to finish.

Wearing a pencil-slim shirtwaist dress and sling-back heels as she was, Megan was hardly dressed for running, but run she did. She ran as though her life depended on it. Her life *did* depend on it If something happened to Swann, it would destroy her.

There was a small but enthusiastic crowd gathered near the stage entrance. They were kept back by a row of brightly painted wooden barricades.

Megan was about thirty yards away when the heavy stage door opened outward. The gathered fans started to whistle and applaud. As Swann stepped out, clad all in black, his eyes hidden by mirrored sunglasses, they went absolutely crazy.

Still running, ignoring the vicious stitch in her side that was shrieking for her to stop, Megan called his name. She poured her heart into the single syllable. She had to. She had almost no breath to give it.

Swann was moving very quickly like a hunting cat on the scent of its prey. He paid no attention to the clamoring throng. Yet, the instant Megan cried out to him, he checked his relentless stride. His dark head snapped in her direction.

Then Megan screamed.

Afterward, when she could analyze it with some shred of objectivity, Megan realized that what happened next took almost less time than she spent brushing her teeth each morning. But while it was actually going on, it had the quality of an endless, slow-motion nightmare.

A young, fair-haired man suddenly detached himself from the crowd of adoring fans and leaped over the barricade. Even at a distance, Megan could see the contorted, hate-filled expression on his face.

Even at a distance, she could see the glint of something sharp and silvery in his right fist.

Then someone else screamed, high, shrill, and hysterical.

The young man lunged for Swann, his right arm coming up.

Swann half turned to confront his attacker, instinctively lifting his own right arm to counter whatever was coming. His swift reflexes and martial arts training probably saved him from serious harm, but they couldn't protect him completely. The young man's arm slashed downward. Swann recoiled, blood showing scarlet on the back of his right hand.

Then everybody seemed to be screaming, including the attacker. He was screaming about Iris Ames. Screaming she was his sister.

Megan never knew what she would have done if Kyle hadn't intervened at that point. Probably something exceedingly dangerous, thanks to the explosion of fear and fury triggered inside her by the sight of Swann's injury.

But Kyle did intervene. Pounding up behind her, he grabbed her and shoved her aside so roughly she lost her balance. She fell to her knees. *"Keep out of this!"* he ordered.

By that time, Swann had already landed a kick on his assailant. The young man staggered, his face savage. Swann dropped fluidly into a defensive posture. The young man snarled and started toward him again.

He never got near Swann. Kyle's tackle prevented it. What the flying leap lacked in finesse, it more than made up for in effectiveness.

It was all over within a few short but horrifyingly violent seconds. When it was, the young man lay stunned on the pavement, a switchblade knife lying about a yard from his slack fingers. Kyle stood over him, rubbing his knuckles.

Suddenly, no one was screaming anymore.

Megan got to her feet. She was shaking with reaction. Her stomach was turning somersaults. Her pantyhose were shredded and her shins were scraped.

None of that mattered.

There was only one thought in her mind . . . one name on her lips . . . one man in her heart.

She reached Swann in nine running steps. She would willingly have run much, much farther, but it wasn't necessary. Swann met her halfway.

Contending with the aftermath of the attack was unpleasant but necessary. After they got through answering questions for the police, there were questions from the press. After they got through answering questions from the press, there were questions from Bernie McGillis, Boomer, Rick, Coney, and Patti.

Then, of course, there were the necessary telephone calls to Swann's mother and Megan's parents. In some ways, the questions from them were the hardest of all.

The story of Swann's assailant came out in sad detail. His name was Richard Ames and he was the brother Iris Ames had been separated from in childhood. He had had emotional problems since being placed in his first foster home, and he'd been in and out of trouble since his early teens. Over the years, he'd become obsessed with the idea of being reunited with his sister. Her refusal to answer any of the letters he'd written to her had triggered a breakdown and he'd been hospitalized for a number of years.

Following his release, he'd decided to go after Swann, the man he blamed for Iris's death.

Swann listened to the tale in silence. Afterward, he'd told Bernie that he wanted to pay for Richard Ames's psychiatric help.

Finally, long past midnight, they were told they could

go home. Standing outside the police station, Megan watched her brother and the man she loved shake hands.

"Thank you," Swann said simply. He appeared tired but alert, his silver-gray eyes brilliant in a face that seemed harder, thinner, and paler than Megan remembered it being five days before. The fleshy part of his right hand was neatly wrapped in a gauze bandage. The wound had looked worse than it was.

"Hey, it's my job," Kyle replied with a quick grin.

Swann smiled back briefly, and then glanced at Megan, who was standing in the sheltering curve of his left arm. "Well, I'm glad you were there to do it," he answered, "but if you ever decide to save my life again, don't shove your sister around to do it."

Megan gazed up at him, knowing her heart was in her eyes. The tenderness in his own expression made her feel utterly cherished. "I'll forgive him this time," she said softly.

There was a pause. It was a lovely, loving silence, full of promises and hope.

"So," Kyle said a little gruffly, "do you two want me to drive you back to Malibu or something? I've got my car. The cops weren't crazy about my abandoning it in the middle of the road as I did, but I managed to talk them out of towing it away after I explained why."

Megan laughed, leaning her head against Swann's strong shoulder. She didn't bother to dispute her younger brother's assumption that she would be going home with Swann. "Swann's got his regular chauffeur back," she said.

"And he believes in keeping his eyes strictly on the road," Swann added, teasing a strand of Megan's red-gold hair for a few seconds between glancing at Kyle. "I hope you understand."

"I get the idea," Kyle conceded. "Well, I guess I'll be moving along then." His eyes moved back and forth between them. "Take care," he said quietly.

"We will, Kyle," Megan replied.

"We'll take care of each other," Swann added.

They said very little to each other during the ride back to Malibu. Words weren't necessary. Perfect communication was possible through looks and touches and smiles.

It was only as the limousine neared the beach house that Swann shifted away from her, his expression serious. "Megan, about what happened the morning after the concert . . . the things I said, the way I treated you. I—it is unforgivable. I don't—"

"No." Shaking her head, she stopped the flow of his words by pressing her fingers gently against his lips. "Not unforgivable. Understandable. If anyone's done anything unforgivable, I'm—I *lied*, Swann."

"You told me you loved me." He kissed her fingers. "That wasn't a lie."

"Then that's all the truth I need from you."

"You told me you loved me, too," she whispered.

"Let me show you how much."

He carried how upstairs to the same room, to the same bed where he had brought her that first night . . . the night she still couldn't remember. After laying her down, he undressed her slowly. When she was completely naked, he stepped back and studied her for several seconds, his eyes moving over her as though he intended to engrave this moment on his heart and memory. Then he stripped off his own clothes and joined her on the bed.

Sexually, they had never been shy with each other. But there was a hint of shyness between them now. Baring their bodies had been blissful, beautiful . . . easy. Baring their souls was equally blissful, equally beautiful . . . but much more difficult.

In the past their lovemaking had been lingering, leisurely, and lazy. It had been fierce, feverish, and fast.

This time it was utterly direct and utterly perfect.

When it was over, Megan knew they had touched in every way possible between man and woman.

"My love, my love," Swann murmured against her hair, fitting her soft, sated body against his.

"My love, my love," she echoed, stroking her fingers over his torso.

"It's tomorrow morning, you know," he told her.

"Tomorrow—" She shifted herself so she could look into his beloved face. It took her only a moment to realize what he meant. "Yes." She smiled. "It *is* tomorrow morning."

It was a time for fresh beginnings. For new hopes and old truths.

Megan tracked the arrogant line of his dark brows with one loving finger. She would never tire of touching him, of being near him. "Swann," she said softly, "you said that my love is the only truth you need from me—"

"It is" he replied, sealing the confirmation with a hot, hard kiss. Her mouth melted like wax against his as she responded.

She broke the caress reluctantly, her cheeks rosy and her eyes glowing. "I—I want you to know the whole story," she declared. "No secrets. I want to tell you what I was going to tell you on that other tomorrow morning."

He smiled tenderly, stroking her curls and taming the silken tangles with his fingers. "You did tell me," he reminded her. "Standing in the living room, burning in the sunlight with the truest, brightest flame imaginable. You did tell me, Megan. But I was too deafened by anger and mistrust to listen. And I was too blinded by my past to realize I was throwing away my future by throwing you out. I was looking at you, but all I could see was myself. My life. I saw myself as a ten-year-old boy surrounded by bodyguards. Scared. Solitary. Separated. With no control over my own life. And I saw myself as a thirty-two-year-old man listening to a woman tell me that everything we'd had between us was a lie... including the son I thought we'd made together."

"Oh, Swann!"

"Shh, love." He hugged her to him. "It's all right, Megan. P.J. is my son in every way that matters. And I'm his father. It's not biology that binds people."

"But to do that to you. To *say* that—"

"It's over. It's finished. Don't you understand? Love, most people only have two choices when it comes to dealing with their past. They can fight it, or they can surrender to it. But, because I have you—what you give me—I can make peace with mine. No more shadows on the present. No more doubts about the future." He paused for a few moments, letting his uninjured left hand flow up her body. His fingers sought the sensitive underside of one of her breasts. The soft globe plumped, its rosy tip pouting under his persuasive attentions. "I was going to come to see you tonight. That was where I was going when Richard—well, when I was leaving the Amphitheater. I did 'Lady Bright' at the end of the last set and then I told the audience there weren't going to be any encores because I had to go find the most important woman in my life."

"Oh, Swann..." She caressed him, feeling a stab of pride as he stiffened under her fingers. "I love you."

"And I love you." Propping himself up on his elbow, he traced the outline of her lips. "So does my son. So much so, that after he got done accusing me of breaking my promise about being good if you came to live with us, he said he was going to stay with my mother until I got you back."

Megan's eyes widened. "Really?"

"Really and truly," he confirmed, quoting one of P.J.'s favorite expressions. "And he took Buddy and Godzilla with him to make the point absolutely clear."

She smiled at him. "Well, you've got me back."

"Not . . . quite."

Her smile faded slightly. "No?"

"I haven't had the chance to tell you what *I* wanted to say on that other tomorrow morning."

Her heart started to pound. She wondered suddenly if it were possible to overdose on happiness. "What was that?"

"Will you marry me, Megan?"

At age thirty, Megan Louise Harper had had a certain amount of experience with getting herself into—and out of—trouble. In some ways, it was fair to say that trouble was her business . . . her family business. Simply put, it took a lot to throw Megan Harper.

How much?

Well, finding herself lying in a familiar bed, in a familiar room, wearing nothing at all while receiving a proposal of marriage from the completely naked rock star who was propped up on one elbow next to her didn't faze her a bit.

But she did blush when she told Swann yes.

SECOND CHANCE AT LOVE

COMING NEXT MONTH

NO MORE MR. NICE GUY #340 by Jeanne Grant
Thinking his fiancée Carroll finds him tame
and predictable, Alan sweeps her away with dashing
recklessness and exotic romance—to her secret
delight...but ultimate dismay!

A PLACE IN THE SUN #341 by Katherine Granger
Libby Peterson hires casual drifter Rush Mason as
groundskeeper for her Cape Cod inn, not anticipating
the exquisite tension provoked by his unexplained
past...or the undisguised passion in his bold gaze.

A PRINCE AMONG MEN #342 by Sherryl Woods
The joke's on mime Erin Matthews when
the devastating man she's spoofing scoops her into
his arms, dubs her his princess—and gives
her ten days to plan their wedding!

NAUGHTY AND NICE #343 by Jan Mathews
Respectable Cindy Marshall's got scars from
when she stripped for a living, and she doesn't need a
man to mess things up now—especially not cool,
compelling vice squad cop Brad Jordan!

ALL THE RIGHT MOVES #344 by Linda Raye
Coach Ryan McFadden is a *big* man, but
five-feet-eleven referee Lauren Nickels is every inch
his equal—whether they're battling it out on
the basketball court...or volleying sexy innuendos.

BLUE SKIES, GOLDEN DREAMS #345 by Kelly Adams
Joe Dancy appears to be an easygoing farmer
with golden good looks and a string of women after him.
Yet Sara Scott's convinced he's after something:
her money...or her heart?

Be Sure to Read These New Releases!

SNOWFLAME #328 by Christa Merlin
Haunted by the conviction that she could have
prevented her husband's death, Elaine Jeffrey finds sweet
comfort in Bruce McClure's passionate embrace, and
together they set out to discover the truth...

BRINGING UP BABY #329 by Diana Morgan
Are the intimate attentions of harried "bachelor father"
George Demarest thanks for Andie Maguire's help with the
scruffy toddler called Speedy. . . or proof of true love?

DILLON'S PROMISE #330 by Cinda Richards
Stunned to learn he's fathered a child by his best friend's
American widow, and haunted by a deathbed promise,
Dillon Cameron storms Thea Kearney's highlands cottage,
intent on claiming "his lasses."

BE MINE, VALENTINE #331 by Hilary Cole
Heiress Melanie Carroway is at her wit's end.
The butler drinks. Her aunt conducts seances.
And dashing Peter Valentine, a charming burglar who steals
only kisses, is trying to seduce her!

SOUTHERN COMFORT #332 by Kit Windham
There's nothing but trouble between brash filmmaker
Leo Myers and cool scriptwriter Kelly Winters. . . until
her sultry sadness prompts him to offer her
the warmest of southern comforts.

NO PLACE FOR A LADY #333 by Cassie Miles
To succeed as the first female professional football player,
Elaine Preston's got to be tough. She can't succumb to
the cynics and critics. . . or to the sexy passes
of big, blond Curt Michaels.

Order on opposite page

SECOND CHANCE AT LOVE

___ 0-425-08673-9	WHISPERS OF AN AUTUMN DAY #305 Lee Williams	$2.25
___ 0-425-08674-7	SHADY LADY #306 Jan Mathews	$2.25
___ 0-425-08675-5	TENDER IS THE NIGHT #307 Helen Carter	$2.25
___ 0-425-08676-3	FOR LOVE OF MIKE #308 Courtney Ryan	$2.25
___ 0-425-08677-1	TWO IN A HUDDLE #309 Diana Morgan	$2.25
___ 0-425-08749-1	LOVERS AND PRETENDERS #310 Liz Grady	$2.25
___ 0-425-08750-6	SWEETS TO THE SWEET #311 Jeanne Grant	$2.25
___ 0-425-08751-4	EVER SINCE EVE #312 Kasey Adams	$2.25
___ 0-425-08752-2	BLITHE SPIRIT #313 Mary Haskell	$2.25
___ 0-425-08753-0	MAN AROUND THE HOUSE #314 Joan Darling	$2.25
___ 0-425-08754-9	DRIVEN TO DISTRACTION #315 Jamisan Whitney	$2.25
___ 0-425-08850-2	DARK LIGHTNING #316 Karen Keast	$2.25
___ 0-425-08851-0	MR. OCTOBER #317 Carole Buck	$2.25
___ 0-425-08852-9	ONE STEP TO PARADISE #318 Jasmine Craig	$2.25
___ 0-425-08853-7	TEMPTING PATIENCE #319 Christina Dair	$2.25
___ 0-425-08854-5	ALMOST LIKE BEING IN LOVE #320 Betsy Osborne	$2.25
___ 0-425-08855-3	ON CLOUD NINE #321 Jean Kent	$2.25
___ 0-425-08908-8	BELONGING TO TAYLOR #322 Kay Robbins	$2.25
___ 0-425-08909-6	ANYWHERE AND ALWAYS #323 Lee Williams	$2.25
___ 0-425-08910-X	FORTUNE'S CHOICE #324 Elissa Curry	$2.25
___ 0-425-08911-8	LADY ON THE LINE #325 Cait Logan	$2.25
___ 0-425-08948-7	A KISS AWAY #326 Sherryl Woods	$2.25
___ 0-425-08949-5	PLAY IT AGAIN, SAM #327 Petra Diamond	$2.25
___ 0-425-08966-5	SNOWFLAME #328 Christa Merlin	$2.25
___ 0-425-08967-3	BRINGING UP BABY #329 Diana Morgan	$2.25
___ 0-425-08968-1	DILLON'S PROMISE #330 Cinda Richards	$2.25
___ 0-425-08969-X	BE MINE, VALENTINE #331 Hilary Cole	$2.25
___ 0-425-08970-3	SOUTHERN COMFORT #332 Kit Windham	$2.25
___ 0-425-08971-1	NO PLACE FOR A LADY #333 Cassie Miles	$2.25
___ 0-425-09117-1	SWANN'S SONG #334 Carole Buck	$2.25
___ 0-425-09118-X	STOLEN KISSES #335 Liz Grady	$2.25
___ 0-425-09119-8	GOLDEN GIRL #336 Jacqueline Topaz	$2.25
___ 0-425-09120-1	SMILES OF A SUMMER NIGHT #337 Delaney Devers	$2.25
___ 0-425-09121-X	DESTINY'S DARLING #338 Adrienne Edwards	$2.25
___ 0-425-09122-8	WILD AND WONDERFUL #339 Lee Williams	$2.25

Available at your local bookstore or return this form to:

SECOND CHANCE AT LOVE
THE BERKLEY PUBLISHING GROUP, Dept. B
390 Murray Hill Parkway, East Rutherford, NJ 07073

Please send me the titles checked above. I enclose _____ Include $1.00 for postage and handling if one book is ordered; 25¢ per book for two or more not to exceed $1.75. New York residents please add sales tax. Prices are subject to change without notice and may be higher in Canada.

NAME _____

ADDRESS _____

CITY _____ STATE/ZIP _____

(Allow six weeks for delivery.)   **SK-41b**

A STIRRING PAGEANTRY
OF
HISTORICAL ROMANCE

Shana Carrol

___ 0-515-08249-X Rebels in Love $3.95

Roberta Gellis

___ 0-515-07529-9 Fire Song $3.95

___ 0-515-08600-2 A Tapestry of Dreams $3.95

Jill Gregory

___ 0-515-07100-5 The Wayward Heart $3.50

___ 0-425-07666-0 My True and Tender Love $6.95
                   (A Berkley Trade Paperback)

___ 0-515-08585-5 Moonlit Obsession $6.95
                   (A Jove Trade Paperback)

___ 0-515-08389-5 Promise Me The Dawn $3.95

Mary Pershall

___ 0-425-07020-4 A Shield of Roses $3.95

Francine Rivers

___ 0-515-08181-7 Sycamore Hill $3.50

___ 0-515-06823-3 This Golden Valley $3.50

Pamela Belle

___ 0-425-08268-7 The Moon in the Water $3.95

___ 0-425-07367-X The Chains of Fate $6.95
                   (A Berkley Trade Paperback)

Shannon Drake

___ 0-515-08637-1 Blue Heaven, Black Night $7.50
                   (A Jove Trade Paperback)

Available at your local bookstore or return this form to:

BERKLEY
THE BERKLEY PUBLISHING GROUP, Dept. B
390 Murray Hill Parkway, East Rutherford, NJ 07073

Please send me the titles checked above. I enclose _____ Include $1.00 for postage and handling if one book is ordered; 25¢ per book for two or more not to exceed $1.75. California, Illinois, New Jersey and Tennessee residents please add sales tax. Prices subject to change without notice and may be higher in Canada.

NAME_____

ADDRESS_____

CITY_____STATE/ZIP_____

(Allow six weeks for delivery.)